He Loves Me Not

Taboo Wedding Series, Volume 1

Lexy Timms

Published by Dark Shadow Publishing, 2019.

This is a work of fiction. Similarities to real people, places, or events are entirely coincidental.

HE LOVES ME NOT

First edition. March 29, 2019.

Copyright © 2019 Lexy Timms.

Written by Lexy Timms.

Also by Lexy Timms

A Burning Love Series
Spark of Passion
Flame of Desire
Blaze of Ecstasy

A Chance at Forever Series
Forever Perfect
Forever Desired
Forever Together

A "Kind of" Billionaire
Taking a Risk
Safety in Numbers
Pretend You're Mine

BBW Romance Series
Capturing Her Beauty
Pursuing Her Dreams

Tracing Her Curves

Beating the Biker Series
Making Her His
Making the Break
Making of Them

Billionaire Banker Series
Banking on Him
Price of Passion
Investing in Love
Knowing Your Worth
Treasured Forever
Banking on Christmas

Billionaire Holiday Romance Series
Driving Home for Christmas
The Valentine Getaway
Cruising Love

Billionaire in Disguise Series
Facade
Illusion
Charade

Billionaire Secrets Series
The Secret
Freedom
Courage
Trust
Impulse
Billionaire Secrets Box Set Books #1-3

Branded Series
Money or Nothing
What People Say
Give and Take

Building Billions
Building Billions - Part 1
Building Billions - Part 2
Building Billions - Part 3

Conquering Warrior Series
Ruthless

Counting the Billions
Counting the Days
Counting On You

Counting the Kisses

Diamond in the Rough Anthology
Billionaire Rock
Billionaire Rock - part 2

Dominating PA Series
Her Personal Assistant - Part 1
Her Personal Assistant Box Set

Fake Billionaire Series
Faking It
Temporary CEO
Caught in the Act
Never Tell A Lie
Fake Christmas

Firehouse Romance Series
Caught in Flames
Burning With Desire
Craving the Heat
Firehouse Romance Complete Collection

For His Pleasure

Elizabeth
Georgia
Madison

Fortune Riders MC Series
Billionaire Biker
Billionaire Ransom
Billionaire Misery

Fragile Series
Fragile Touch
Fragile Kiss
Fragile Love

Hades' Spawn Motorcycle Club
One You Can't Forget
One That Got Away
One That Came Back
One You Never Leave
One Christmas Night
Hades' Spawn MC Complete Series

Hard Rocked Series
Rhyme
Harmony
Lyrics

Heart of Stone Series
The Protector
The Guardian
The Warrior

Heart of the Battle Series
Celtic Viking
Celtic Rune
Celtic Mann
Heart of the Battle Series Box Set

Heistdom Series
Master Thief
Goldmine
Diamond Heist
Smile For Me

Just About Series
About Love
About Truth
About Forever

Justice Series
Seeking Justice

Finding Justice
Chasing Justice
Pursuing Justice
Justice - Complete Series

Kissed by Billions
Kissed by Passion
Kissed by Desire
Kissed by Love

Love You Series
Love Life
Need Love
My Love

Managing the Billionaire
Never Enough
Worth the Cost
Secret Admirers
Chasing Affection
Pressing Romance
Timeless Memories

Managing the Bosses Series
The Boss
The Boss Too

Who's the Boss Now
Love the Boss
I Do the Boss
Wife to the Boss
Employed by the Boss
Brother to the Boss
Senior Advisor to the Boss
Forever the Boss
Christmas With the Boss
Billionaire in Control
Billionaire Makes Millions
Billionaire at Work
Precious Little Thing
Priceless Love
Gift for the Boss - Novella 3.5
Managing the Bosses Box Set #1-3

Model Mayhem Series
Shameless
Modesty
Imperfection

Moment in Time
Highlander's Bride
Victorian Bride
Modern Day Bride
A Royal Bride
Forever the Bride

Neverending Dream Series
Neverending Dream - Part 1
Neverending Dream - Part 2
Neverending Dream - Part 3
Neverending Dream - Part 4

Outside the Octagon
Submit
Fight
Knockout

Protecting Diana Series
Her Bodyguard
Her Defender
Her Champion
Her Protector
Her Forever

Protecting Layla Series
His Mission
His Objective
His Devotion

Racing Hearts Series

Rush
Pace
Fast

Reverse Harem Series
Primals
Archaic
Unitary

RIP Series
Track the Ripper
Hunt the Ripper
Pursue the Ripper

R&S Rich and Single Series
Alex Reid
Parker

Saving Forever
Saving Forever - Part 1
Saving Forever - Part 2
Saving Forever - Part 3
Saving Forever - Part 4
Saving Forever - Part 5
Saving Forever - Part 6
Saving Forever Part 7

Saving Forever - Part 8
Saving Forever Boxset Books #1-3

Shifting Desires Series
Jungle Heat
Jungle Fever
Jungle Blaze

Southern Romance Series
Little Love Affair
Siege of the Heart
Freedom Forever
Soldier's Fortune

Spanked Series
Passion
Playmate
Pleasure

Spelling Love Series
The Author
The Book Boyfriend
The Words of Love

Taboo Wedding Series
He Loves Me Not
With This Ring
Happily Ever After

Tattooist Series
Confession of a Tattooist
Surrender of a Tattooist
Heart of a Tattooist
Hopes & Dreams of a Tattooist

Tennessee Romance
Whisky Lullaby
Whisky Melody
Whisky Harmony

The Bad Boy Alpha Club
Battle Lines - Part 1
Battle Lines

The Brush Of Love Series
Every Night
Every Day
Every Time

Every Way
Every Touch

The Debt
The Debt: Part 1 - Damn Horse
The Debt: Complete Collection

The Golden Mail
Hot Off the Press
Extra! Extra!

The University of Gatica Series
The Recruiting Trip
Faster
Higher
Stronger
Dominate
No Rush
University of Gatica - The Complete Series

T.N.T. Series
Troubled Nate Thomas - Part 1
Troubled Nate Thomas - Part 2
Troubled Nate Thomas - Part 3

Undercover Series
Perfect For Me
Perfect For You
Perfect For Us

Unknown Identity Series
Unknown
Unpublished
Unexposed
Unsure
Unwritten
Unknown Identity Box Set: Books #1-3

Unlucky Series
Unlucky in Love
UnWanted
UnLoved Forever

Wet & Wild Series
Stormy Love
Savage Love
Secure Love

Worth It Series

Worth Billions
Worth Every Cent
Worth More Than Money

You & Me - A Bad Boy Romance
Just Me
Touch Me
Kiss Me

Standalone
Wash
Loving Charity
Summer Lovin'
Love & College
Billionaire Heart
First Love
Frisky and Fun Romance Box Collection
Beating Hades' Bikers

Watch for more at www.lexytimms.com.

USA TODAY BESTSELLING AUTHOR
LEXY TIMMS

HE LOVES ME Not

Copyright 2019

ALL RIGHTS RESERVED. No part of this publication may be reproduced, stored in or introduced into a retrieval system, or transmitted, in any form, or by any means (electronic, mechanical, photocopying, recording, or otherwise) without the prior written permission of both the copyright owner and the above publisher of this book.

This is a work of fiction. Names, characters, places, brands, media, and incidents are either the product of the author's imagination or are used fictitiously. Any resemblance to an actual person, living or dead, events, or locales is entirely coincidental. The author acknowledges the trademarked status and trademark owners of various products referenced in this work of fiction, which have been used without permission. The publication/use of these trademarks is not authorized, associated with, or sponsored by the trademark owners.

All rights reserved.
He Loves Me Not
Taboo Wedding Series #1
Copyright 2019 by Lexy Timms
Cover by: Book Cover by Design[1]

---

1. http://bookcoverbydesign.co.uk/

Taboo Wedding Series

Book 1 – He Loves Me Not
Book 2 – With This Ring
Book 3 – Happily Ever After
"A romance story yet to be written."

Find Lexy Timms:

LEXY TIMMS NEWSLETTER:
http://eepurl.com/9i0vD
Lexy Timms Facebook Page:
https://www.facebook.com/SavingForever
Lexy Timms Website:
http://www.lexytimms.com

Want to read more...
For **FREE?**
Sign up for Lexy Timms' newsletter
At your request, she'll send you updates on new releases, ARC copies of books and a whole lotta fun!
Sign up for news and updates!
http://eepurl.com/9i0vD

He Loves Me Not - Blurb

"WE CRAVE WHAT WE CAN'T have...

When you have a chance to plan the wedding of all weddings, falling for the gorgeous groom is out of the question. How does one ignore the sparks, the attraction, and the forbidden fruit right in front of them?

Trying to keep her head down, Lilac Freesia (yes, her mother had a bad sense of humor) just wants to get the job done and pretend she doesn't feel anything.

Except, what if she can't walk away from the job of a lifetime—or the man of her dreams?

"But you can't control who you love."

Chapter One

"Violet, are you listening to me?"

I forced my attention away from the breathtaking sight framed by the round airplane window. We were flying over an ocean bluer than anything I had seen before, not a cloud in the sky to impede the view. Before that moment, the only ocean I'd ever seen had been the dull gray Atlantic along the New York shoreline. It had certainly never been so mesmerizing.

"I'm sorry, Nathaniel." I put on a smile and turned to face my boss. "It's a little distracting."

He waved the apology away. "I'm sure it's quite a sight your first time. But do keep in mind, dear, that I need you to focus. This is a job. Not your vacation."

The words were mild, but there was a bite to his tone. I swallowed the sigh I wanted to exhale and made myself smile wider. It probably looked pretty fake; I'd never been great at putting on a facade. But then, I was learning a whole lot about make believe working with Nathaniel.

I'd been working in event planning for almost two years before I got the job with Nathaniel, and I'd thought I knew about the business, but weddings were an entirely different thing. Even the ones you wanted most to believe were fairytale moments were one part reality and nine parts illusion, and wedding planners were the ones who put that all together and made it look seamless. We were the ones responsible for the image of perfect, even if it was nothing but chaos beneath the surface.

Which was not to say that I didn't appreciate the chance to work with Nathaniel. It was the chance of a lifetime. He was an up-and-coming name in a fiercely competitive business, and the destination wedding we were on our way to was as high-profile as they came. Both families were stars in the New York stratosphere, the kind of high society who showed up in glossy photos next to movie stars. Rich enough to fly the wedding planner and his new assistant to a private Caribbean island owned by a billionaire friend of the family.

The truth was, as much as I knew I had to remain professional, excitement bubbled in my chest. But I was determined to keep it on a tight rein. The career opportunity here was huge, and not just for Nathaniel. If I handled it right, I'd be set.

"You seem a bit overwhelmed," Nathaniel said, cutting into my thoughts with an edge that said he'd noticed my distraction again.

He wasn't wrong. I was definitely starting to feel like I was in a little over my head, and I hadn't even met the happy couple yet. Since he'd brought me in at practically the last second, I wouldn't have a face-to-face with the wedding party until we arrived on the island.

I was also completely exhausted. Nathaniel had received my résumé from a friend of a friend, and took me on at their recommendation only a few days ago. He interviewed me once, and offered me the job on the spot. It felt like I hadn't stopped running since.

"Not... overwhelmed," I answered. *Just overworked.*

"I'm take a huge chance with you, Violet. This wedding is my biggest event of the year, and it's hardly possible to take someone else on at this point." He ran a hand through his already-tousled dark hair the way he always did when he was frazzled. "After Elizabeth I needed someone honest, and heaven knows you can't lie to save your life. But you have to be more than just that if you're going to actually be useful."

If he'd been a little more well known, his previous assistant's firing and arrest for embezzlement would have been a tabloid headline. As it was, it meant he'd been desperate for a replacement, and I'd been in the right place at the right time to cash in on the opportunity. I was honestly pretty sure he wouldn't have hired me under any other circumstances, but I wasn't about to look a gift horse in the mouth. Whatever that means.

I had a hospitality degree. It wasn't from a great college, and I'd spent more time waitressing in the last three years than I had in event planning, but I still had qualifications. Just not the kind good enough to get me a spot with a man like Nathaniel Lamond without a minor miracle involved.

"I know you are," I said, and I meant it. "And I'm incredibly grateful for the opportunity."

"Then stop mooning over the view and listen." Nathaniel opened the leather-bound notebook he carried with him everywhere and started shuffling through papers, reading glasses perched on the end of his nose. "We land in about an hour. You'll have time to freshen up in your room, and then I'll need you ready to work. Here." He handed me a printed map that was a bewildering array of shapes all neatly labeled with numbers. And then he dropped a wireless microphone on top of the map. "Wear this. I don't want to see you without it."

That, at least, I recognized. I picked up the mic and slipped it into place, feeling for the on/off button.

"This is quite the place." I studied the map, trying to familiarize myself with the pastel-colored shapes. "Who did you say owns the island again?"

It was Nathaniel's turn to sigh. "Bartholomew Court. You *have* heard of him. He owns this island and several others. A bit eccentric, but..." He grinned at me, his teeth impeccably white. "Aren't they all?"

Present company included, I thought, although I was reasonably sure at least part of it was a show he put on for the clients. He was definitely more on the serious side when the two of us were alone together.

"This—" Nathanial tapped on the map with a manicured fingernail, "is Pearl Island. It's all written down."

Another paper fluttered into my lap.

"Ah. Okay. Got it." Or I hoped I did. I found my room and the main villa on the map, tracing a line between the two. It was a *very* long line. I swallowed another sigh. Best guess was at least a twenty-minute walk from point A to point B.

As though he could read my mind, Nathaniel said, "There will be a golf cart for you to use."

Better than nothing, I supposed.

"Here's the information on the families. You'll have gone over it already, I don't doubt—it was in the information packet I gave you—but it pays to be prepared. Read over it again before we touch down. You'll be responsible for greeting some of the guests and taking them to their villas, so you'll want to have a firm grasp on this list." He shoved it at me. "The bride and groom, of course, I'll handle myself."

The guest list in my hand was three pages long. And that, as far as I could tell, was just relatives. My own extended family barely filled the first few rows of any church. This had my mind reeling.

"I'll expect you to have at least a general idea of which name goes with which picture. They're all the groom's side. The bride's immediate family is only her mother. Which is a rather sad story."

I flipped open the folder. At the top was a photograph of the bride and groom—their engagement photo, by the looks of it.

The bride, Emeline Brant, rested her head on the groom's broad shoulder. She was tall, almost taller than he was, willowy and copper-haired, her smile just a touch less dazzling than the diamond engagement ring she was trying very hard to showcase. Her left hand rested stiffly on her groom's chest, the ring tilted toward the camera.

And the groom... Raymond Rose. It was a name almost as ridiculous as my own. And it certainly didn't suit the face I was looking at.

He was incredibly good-looking, his short hair a sun-bleached blond that complemented his golden tan. His arm was around the bride's shoulder, and they made a very good-looking couple in a very upper class, 'tennis-whites-on-weekends at the country club' kind of way.

His smile, I noted, was more reserved than Emeline's. He looked at the camera with a strong, steady gaze, a kind of quiet confidence radiating from him. It spoke of something beyond sparkling baby blues and a handsome face.

I'd seen photos of him before, of course, in the society pages. My roommate and I had become a little obsessed with hunting down information about him and his bride since I got hired. But those hadn't seemed so... intimate. Here, he had the kind of eyes that looked at you and then *into* you. The kind of look that, against your better judgment, would take your breath away, leaving you reminiscing about your first awkward kiss and wondering what it would have been like if you were with someone like him.

All that from a photograph? I chided myself. *Pull it together, Violet.*

I ran my finger slowly over his image. He was a prince, with his princess, looking forward to a fairytale wedding. But if that was the case, why didn't the smile on his face reach all the way up into those impossibly blue eyes?

Chapter Two

The plane touched down, bouncing lightly on the runway, and rolling to a smooth stop in front of a small glass-fronted building that appeared to serve as a terminal. The door sprang open and we were instantly greeted by an older man, short and stocky, wearing a Hawaiian shirt, khaki shorts, and a wide-brimmed hat. I blinked in the bright sunlight as I descended from the plane, not quite sure of what I was seeing. It definitely was not what I would have expected from a man rich enough to own his own island. But then, I supposed if you were that rich you could wear whatever you damn well pleased. He hurried toward us and Nathaniel stepped forward ahead of me, wearing his professional business smile.

"Mr. Lamond, I presume. It's so nice to finally meet you in person." He shook Nathaniel's hand before turning to me.

"And—oh, I'm sorry, dear. I don't know your name." The English accent was cheerful and it made me smile. I accepted his outstretched hand.

"Violet." I hesitated as I always did when I had to give my full name. "Violet Freesia."

He stared at me, the way most people did.

"My mother had a questionable sense of humor."

"Well, Violet is a lovely name in any case," he said, recovering quickly. He gave my hand a hearty shake and then stepped back, rubbing his hands together, his face wreathed in a huge smile. I liked him immediately. I'd been a bit intimidated by the thought of meeting a billionaire who owned his own island—island*s*—but so far, so good.

"I'm Bartholomew Court. Welcome to Pearl Island." He waved an arm at the glittering terminal and the glimpse of lush foliage beyond. "I like to greet all my guests personally, if I can. And I'm so excited that you're here to help with the planning of this extraordinary wedding for our lovely couple. I've known Ray since he was just a boy."

He turned, moving toward the building. "They haven't arrived yet—due later today. Come with me... I have all the information you'll need."

I knew Nathaniel had all the arrival information, down to the last second. It was outlined in scrupulous detail in the folders we both carried, but he deferred to Mr. Court, something I'd rarely seen him do with anyone. I followed them as we walked across the tarmac.

Beyond the glass doors of the terminal, our pilot was busy chatting with a pretty young woman sitting at a desk. A few other people walked briskly here and there, obviously sure where they were going, but otherwise it was unexpectedly calm.

"Here it is." He shuffled papers on a desk and finally produced a printed sheet. He promptly handed it to Nathaniel, who scanned the page with a quick glance.

"Violet will be handling the transport of guests to their villas once they've arrived," he said. "I have everything else to organize."

"Brilliant." Court turned to me, practically beaming. "Then I shall be seeing a great deal of you today, my dear." He motioned to someone behind us. "Andrea will take you to your respective rooms and help get you settled. Violet, I'll see you back here shortly."

And with that, Andrea, a tall woman with short dark hair, dressed in impeccable white linen, promptly whisked us out the door. Our bags followed in the hands of a couple of uniformed men.

The sun was hot as we stepped out of the small building, but the view took my breath away. From the air, the island was nothing more than a dot of green with an edge of golden sand beach. But here, up close, it really was a paradise.

Deeply-shaded paths headed off in several directions, and I was relieved to see discrete signs pointing the way to different villas and buildings. Andrea quickly loaded our luggage and we climbed into what had to be the largest golf cart I'd ever seen. Painted a pale blue with *Pearl Island* stamped in elegant lettering on the side, it resembled a mini Hummer, complete with the wide chrome grill and shiny rims.

If I'd had any trepidation about driving a golf cart to begin with, it certainly doubled now. This thing was a behemoth compared to the little carts I'd seen bumping along at the public golf courses. It could easily hold six people, plus luggage. And ford a river if necessary.

I tried to lean forward and watch what Andrea was doing with the controls, but I'd been relegated to the back seat and couldn't really see much of what was going on up front. So I settled back and tried to focus on enjoying the view, hoping that I'd be able to figure it all out later on. I was a quick study, but that didn't mean I wasn't worried.

Incredibly beautiful flowers in a rainbow of colors bordered the paths between villas, a riot of blooms against the green of palms and other tropical trees. Birds flitted through the foliage, making all kinds of exotic noises.

"There's been a change of plans," Nathaniel said. He held out the sheet Bartholomew had given him. "Apparently the bride and groom are arriving on separate flights, instead of together. I'm not certain why someone didn't call me, but this means I'll have to take Emeline to her villa and you'll take Ray to his."

"That's fine," I said, trying to steady the hint of panic that had crept into Nathaniel's voice. "Not a problem at all."

"I just can't leave one in the terminal waiting for me," he said, still tense, and I was reminded that I wasn't the only one on new footing. He'd never done a wedding like this before.

"I understand, Nathaniel. Really. I'm fine taking the groom to his villa." Or I would be fine, once I figured out how to work the golf cart. Maybe I could convince Andrea to give me a quick lesson.

We pulled up in front of a small building with a sign on the door labeling it the *Palm Villa*. I wondered if it was Nathaniel's or mine. My trusty map was safely tucked away at the moment, but the answer was soon made clear as Nathaniel climbed out of the cart and Andrea retrieved his luggage from the back.

"I'm the wedding planner," Nathaniel said, leaning back into the cart as Andrea climbed the steps of the villa. "They know me and expect to see my face. Not yours. Emeline is somewhat high-strung and I don't want her upset."

"Which is why you're taking Emeline and I'm taking the groom." I hopped out of the back seat of the cart, moving up to the front so I could eye the control panel. "I'll be on my best behavior. I promise."

Andrea emerged from the villa, sliding into the driver's seat of the cart. "You're all set, Mr. Lamond. There's a guest phone if you need anything. Just dial zero for the staff office. Someone will be by in half an hour, as you requested, to take you to the main villa."

"Plans changed," Nathaniel said. "I'm going to the terminal, not the villa. Please see that whoever is picking me up is made aware." He turned back to me. "You need to be unobtrusive. Remember that. You're an assistant, and assistants are meant to fade into the background. Keep your microphone turned on, and I expect you at the terminal in thirty minutes."

He turned and headed up to the villa, discussion closed. My hand lifted to my ear and I clicked the small button on the headpiece, a burst of static announcing its awakening. Andrea watched Nathaniel's retreating back for a moment, her face impassive, before she turned to me and broke into a smile.

"Are you ready for your driving lesson?"

I smiled back at her, unable to resist the contagious expression. "How did you know I needed one?"

"I heard your boss say you were going to be transporting guests. And I also saw the look on your face when you saw this thing." She chuckled, the corners of her mouth and eyes etched with the signs of years of good humor.

"I've been told I should never play poker," I admitted, relaxing against my seat. "So what's the trick to handling one of these?"

"The only thing you really need to remember is to plug it in at night. It's electric. If you don't do that, you're in for a lot of walking."

"Got it. Plug it in every night. What else?" I leaned forward, watching intently.

"Key to start." She pointed to a small key stuck in the dash, turned it, and the motor purred to life. "Simple. You've driven a car?"

I nodded.

"Gas on the right, brake is the big pedal on the left. And..." She pointed to her feet. I looked down and laughed. The pedal on the right was emblazoned with GO in big letters. The brake bore a matching STOP.

"Wonderful. I think I can manage that." My nerves were dissipating. "It kind of looks like fun."

"You want to drive?"

My mouth dropped open. "Really?"

"No better way to learn."

"Yeah. Yeah. I'd love that."

We exchanged places, and Andrea showed me how to adjust the seat so I had at least a fighting chance of reaching the pedals. The gearshift was in the dash by my left hand, and she guided me into shifting it into drive. After a jerky start, I made a wide turn in the clearing of the villa and headed off at barely more than walking speed down the narrow path.

"It's easier when you get to the wider paths," she said. "These paths up to the villas are way too small. Here, turn right."

I did as I was told, carefully turning where Andrea pointed, and the path widened.

"Give it some gas. Top speed is just under twenty miles an hour, but you'll have no reason to go that fast. At a safe speed, braking distance is about ten feet or so. Test it out. See what it's like."

I tapped the brake, and the cart responded immediately. It was easier than I'd thought it would be, and I said as much.

Andrea smiled. "They're not nearly as intimidating as they look," she agreed.

With Andrea directing me we headed down the path, curving around a rocky outcrop, and pulled up in front of my villa. Andrea slid out of the cart, which was parked next to a matching vehicle I assumed was the cart I would be driving, and grabbed my bags from the back.

"You're further from the action than I thought you'd be," she said as I got out of the cart. "But maybe it's because there are so many guests for the wedding. Although there are bigger staff quarters available." I didn't miss the tone in her voice or the way her eyebrows drew together.

I shrugged. "I don't need a whole lot of space. Coming from a New York City apartment with a roommate, this is huge. Besides, I'm working. How much time am I really going to be spending here?"

She laughed. "Fair enough. And better to make the best of it."

I followed her up the wide steps to the villa, noticing there was no sign indicating a name for my pied-a-terre. It probably wasn't big enough to have one. Or maybe none of the staff quarters did. Nathaniel's had, but they could have put him in a guest house.

Andrea set my bags down inside the door, and I peered around her. The room was actually quite nice, although it was small, mostly dominated by a huge bed with a gauzy white canopy and curtains. But that wasn't what caught my attention.

"I'm right on the beach," I realized, looking out at crystal blue waters through the windows along the back wall.

"One of the perks of being on the back end of the island," Andrea answered.

I threw open the French doors, the curtains fluttering in the warm breeze, and drew in a deep breath. It smelled divine, like salt and sand and the rich perfume of the flowers. For the space of that breath, I forgot everything but the tropical paradise I was standing in.

"I need to get back to the terminal," Andrea said, breaking the spell of the moment. "I think you're due back there as well. Do you want to follow me, or can I trust you to find your own way?"

I reluctantly turned from the view, taking one last breath of fresh ocean air. "I think I'll be fine. I have a map somewhere. Just show me how to unplug the cart and I'll be good to go. And thank you, Andrea. For all of your help."

"Call me Andi," she answered, lips curving up.

We stepped outside, and she gave me a brief explanation of how the cart plug worked, then left in a hurry, rushing off to take care of yet another errand. I took my map and went back to my ocean view.

There were two deck chairs outside the French doors and I plopped down in one, sinking into the cushions. I really was isolated. According to the map, the nearest villas were assigned to the groom and his party. And although they weren't far cross country, or by walking on the beach, they were quite a distance via the paths. I found the terminal on the map, made some notes in the margins, and went back to the front porch of my room and down the steps.

"Well," I said, staring at the golf cart. "It's just you and me."

Remembering Andi's instructions, I unplugged it. Then I climbed in and turned the key, and the engine purred to life.

"Yeah, here we go." I managed to turn the cart around, less gracefully than Andi would have, but still it got me out onto the main path. At something slightly faster than a snail's pace, I headed back toward the terminal. The paths all looked the same, but I diligently followed my map and the glass-fronted building finally came into sight.

I parked and noticed one other cart already in the small area outside the building. Once inside, I realized it belonged to Nathaniel. He was standing at the other side of the room, staring out at the tarmac.

"Any sign of the bride?" I stood next to him, watching the tarmac shimmering in the heat, the palms waving overhead. The polyester jacket I really should have changed out of when we arrived was already sticking to my back, and I surreptitiously undid the top button.

"No, not yet. But the groom's plane is just coming into view." He pointed and I saw a tiny silver speck in the deep blue sky. We watched it grow larger and then it landed, sending up small dust clouds as the wheels hit the tarmac. The sleek private jet taxied up to the building, coming to a quick stop.

"Do you still want me to take him to his villa?"

Bartholomew had walked out of the terminal and stood waiting in the sun, his hat casting his face in shadow. But I knew that big smile was in place. His entire body practically thrummed with excitement.

Nathaniel shrugged, an upward heave of one shoulder under the deep blue silk of his shirt. "I have no choice. Emeline is... under a lot of pressure. This may upset her and I want to be there for her, to keep things under control."

I nodded. The steps lowered down from the side of the jet and a man began descending. He stopped halfway, turned back, and spoke briefly to someone inside, his face obscured by the wing of the plane. Then he stepped into the bright sun.

Even at a distance he was striking. His hair was longer than in the photograph, the sun setting off golden highlights, and the breeze ruffled it like a lover's hand, sending a few stray strands across his forehead. He looked relaxed and casual, striding toward the terminal in khakis and a white cotton shirt. And he looked incredibly happy, as I guess all grooms should look on the eve of their wedding.

Bartholomew greeted him, not with a handshake but with a full-on hug. I wondered what the connection was between the two, between the families.

"Violet? I asked if you're okay with this."

I turned to Nathaniel, meeting his expectant look, my work smile firmly in place.

"I'm fine, yes. I know where I'm going and I've mastered the golf cart, so I'm good to go. What about his luggage?"

"Throw it in the cart," Nathaniel said with another unconcerned shrug. He was putting on the attitude he used around clients—languid and impossible to ruffle. "And try to stay focused, would you? Running the cart into a tree would be just the kind of disaster I'm trying to avoid."

The doors whisked open before I could answer and the groom walked through, escorted by Bartholomew, who deposited him in front of us before discretely stepping back. I thought he gave me a wink, but between his hat and the sudden presence of the groom I may have been mistaken.

The groom, Raymond Rose. I held back a sigh and found a smile. A genuine smile this time. *Nothing fake here.*

Nathaniel was stepping forward, a hand extended to catch Raymond Rose's. "Ray," he said, smiling like he didn't have a care in the world. He was much better at faking it than I was. "Good to see you."

"A pleasure as always, Nathaniel."

He was taller than he'd appeared in the photograph. Tall enough that Nathaniel had to look up at him. He pulled away and turned his smile on me. My face grew hot. In this light, his eyes were the exact same color of the ocean outside my room.

"Sorry for the change in plans," he said, looking at me but talking to Nathaniel. "They had a surprise last day of work luncheon for Emeline, and I was stuck in the city on business."

"It's no trouble," Nathaniel answered. "I know how you New York City socialite types are." He laughed. "Frankly, I would have been more surprised if the schedule *didn't* get a slight hiccup in at some point. My assistant will take you to your villa so you can get settled and rest a little, and when Emeline arrives I'll conduct her to hers."

"Great. Thanks." Ray was still looking at me, an open and expectant look on his face.

I stepped forward, hand extended. His closed around it and I tried to ignore the warmth of it, the solid strength of his grip. This was my client. Someone else's husband-to-be. I had no business thinking about how comfortable his hand felt in mine.

"I'm Violet," I said when I realized the silence had gone on long enough to be awkward. "I'll be your chauffeur for today."

His smile deepened, and I looked up into those eyes I'd seen in the photo. The ones that had so startled me when he first walked in. They looked darker now, so close, but just as intense. I swallowed the inappropriate sigh that wanted to escape and let go of his hand.

"Your chariot awaits."

Ray stepped ahead and held the door for me as we walked out into the bright afternoon. Andi was already outside, directing a couple guys who were loading Ray's luggage into the cart.

"This our ride?" he asked.

I nodded.

"It's cool," he said. "How does it handle?"

He looked at me and I shrugged. "Not sure I got it past walking speed, to be honest. This is my first time with one of these."

"Do you mind if I drive? Is that breaking any kind of wedding planner rule?" He smiled, revealing a dimple that made my heart threaten to stop in my chest, and I helplessly smiled back. "I won't tell if you don't."

"You're the guy in charge," I said. "I can't refuse a request as simple as getting to drive your own golf cart." I climbed into the passenger seat as Ray got behind the wheel, and looked up to find him watching me, his blue eyes fixed on my face. My cheeks heated once more. "But, just in case, it can be our little secret."

"Cross your heart and hope to die," Ray laughed. He turned the key and looked over at me. "Ready?"

"Ready."

"Hang on," he advised. And then we were off.

I have no idea how fast twenty miles an hour is in a golf cart, but I suspect we were going at least that fast. I managed to point with one hand while clutching the seat with the other and we finally arrived at Ray's villa, unscathed.

Ray, when I turned to look at him, was beaming like a little boy with a new toy. "I need to get one of these."

"I'm not sure your new bride would appreciate you putting yourself in that kind of danger," I answered, and won another laugh from him. My heart fluttered in my chest.

"Hold still," he said abruptly, reaching toward me.

I froze, squeezing my eyes shut. "Is it a spider?" My heart had gone from breathless fluttering to skittering erratically in my chest.

"No. Just..." I felt his fingers brush across my forehead. I opened my eyes. "Your hair. It got a little windblown. Sorry." He was leaning forward in his seat, smiling, holding my gaze. I wanted to make a witty comeback but sat frozen instead, lips parted in silence. All my words seemed to have abandoned me in the wake of his touch.

"Are you afraid of bugs?" He sat back in his seat then and that tiny moment—the flicker of connection between us—broke apart. I found my voice.

"Not bugs...spiders. There's a difference, you know. Bugs are a dime a dozen in New York. But spiders..." I shivered dramatically. "Not my thing."

He laughed and it was a nice sound. I had no choice but to smile back. "Sorry to say it, but you're probably going to run into a few here. What with it being a tropical island and everything."

"I'm trying not to think about that, if you don't mind," I retorted, very much trying not to now that he'd mentioned it. "Do you want to see your villa?" I pointed to a sign along the path. "It even has a name."

We got out of the cart, heading up the steps to the villa, which was painted in rich green and royal blue, likely to go with its name: the *Bird of Paradise.*

Ray opened the door. I stepped inside and stopped dead in my tracks.

It was much larger than my own little place further around the curve of the island, the walls paneled in dark mahogany that seemed to glow softly in the sunlight that spilled through the open door. Gauzy white curtains were hung along the floor-to-ceiling windows. In the center was a sunken living room, taken up with white linen-covered, wooden-framed chairs and benches arranged in casual groupings. It had to be seating for at least twenty people. Beyond, doors led off to other rooms. Many other rooms. I thought again of my single room with its little bathing area.

Ray laughed, taking my arm and pulling me gently down the stairs into the center of the room. "Look," he said, pointing.

I looked up and drew in a breath, my eyes widening. "Wow. This must be fantastic at night." The ceiling of the two-story room was nothing but one large sheet of glass, the brilliant blue sky stretching out above it like something out of a movie set.

"It is. The stars look like they're right in the room with you."

He was still looking up at the ceiling when I turned to glance at him. His profile was an example of chiseled masculinity. His mouth, though, was full and soft, and I couldn't help but notice again the dimple that appeared when he smiled.

"Wow," I breathed. Truth be told, I wasn't entirely talking about the view overhead. And then the actual meaning of his words struck me. "So... you've been in this villa before?"

"Yeah," he admitted, finally turning to look at me. He smiled a little sheepishly, running a hand through his wind-blown hair. "My family and Bartholomew's go way back. My grandfather and his father were quite the pair in London, if you believe their stories. They're still banned from several gentlemen's clubs, for various reasons, none of which have ever been clearly explained to us."

His laugh was brief. "I should have told you, I guess, that I knew how to get here. To the villa, I mean. But you were having so much fun being my tour guide that I didn't want to interrupt. Sorry if that comes off as kind of misleading."

"I can forgive you, since you stopped me before I embarrassed myself too thoroughly." I smiled at him. "I was going to give you this whole spiel about the island, and you probably know more about it than I ever will."

He rubbed at the back of his neck. "I probably do. For what it's worth, though, the carts are new. And I really had a great time driving one. Thank you."

"We should get your luggage," I said, because I was afraid that if I didn't I might have let something I really shouldn't have slip.

"Probably a good plan," he agreed.

We unloaded the bags, hauling them up the steps to the villa. As we finished, there was a crackle of static in my ear and I jumped, hand flying up in a vain attempt to turn down the volume on the ear piece. And then Nathaniel's voice was there, loud and clear, instructing me to return to the terminal. Immediately. Ray gave me a quizzical look.

"I need to go." I gave him my professional hospitality-degree smile and extended my hand once more. Formalities and introductions were over, but I wanted one last chance to feel his hand in mine. A pinprick of guilt stabbed me; this was someone's—Emeline's—future husband.

But he was also one of the nicest men I'd met in a long time, and one of the best looking. One more handshake would hold me for a long time. Princes didn't come along very often, even in the guise of millionaire businessmen. "It's been a pleasure meeting you, Ray. Please, if there's anything you need, let Nathaniel or me know."

He reached out in return and I felt the warmth of his skin, the solid weight of his hand in mine. I thought about Emeline, the princess to his prince. She was one lucky girl. I wondered if she knew just how lucky.

"Thank you, Violet," he said as he withdrew his touch. "And thanks for letting me drive the Hummer."

"Our secret, remember," I said.

"I won't tell Nathaniel if you don't," he returned, a conspiratorial grin on his face.

I tried to stifle a laugh and didn't succeed, finally giving in and letting it wash over me. It felt good to laugh; life had been a bit on the serious side lately.

"Call if you need anything," I repeated when I'd managed to pull myself together. "Emeline should be here soon, and the rest of your groomsmen are scheduled to arrive later. Oh, and there's a dinner party tonight at the main villa."

Ray walked me to the door. "Yeah, I know. I'm looking forward to getting together with the guys, that's for sure. Been too long. It was supposed to be a sort of bachelor party, but somehow that got changed in the final plans to a more formal dinner. But seeing everyone, my friends and family, especially my grandparents, is going to be great."

"And seeing Emeline..." I glanced up at Ray. He was looking out the door, across to the green palms and tangle of flowers outside his villa. The smile on his face faded just the slightest bit, his expression dimming as though a cloud had passed across his eyes. I was reminded again of the engagement photograph, the smile that didn't quite seem real.

But when he looked back at me the smile was back in place, the eyes bright. "And Emeline. Yes, of course."

On the ride back to the terminal, the wind in my hair now that I discovered I could go fast without crashing, I thought about illusions. There are the ones we construct for ourselves, to make our lives easier and to get through the day, content with living in blind bliss.

And then there are the illusions we construct for the rest of the world, to make others see us as we want to be seen, or as they wish to see us.

Fairy-tale weddings are always an illusion in one way or another. But in this case it seemed like more than that. In this case, I thought maybe the illusion was the relationship itself.

Chapter Three

I walked into absolute chaos at the terminal. Nathaniel, looking more nonplussed than I'd ever seen him, was clutching his notebook at the edge of a group of women, most of them talking at once. In the center was the red-haired woman I assumed was Emeline, sobbing into the rigid arms of a statuesque older woman, who appeared to be attempting to console the bride without actually touching her. Unless I was very mistaken, she was the woman I remembered from the photographs as the bride's mother.

The bridesmaids—or at least I assumed that was who they were—fluttered closer in turn, each of them brushing a hand along the bride's arm or shoulder or over her hair, whispering what I assumed was meant to be comfort. A couple of them stood back at the edge of the rest, exchanging glances.

Even Bartholomew looked at a loss. He was standing off to the side with a subdued group of island employees. I saw Andi among them, her expression as impassive as ever, but I thought if I looked closely there was something a little pitying in the turn of her mouth.

"You can stop this any minute now, Emeline. There are other people present." I'd never actually heard anyone hiss before, but the sound the woman made as she spoke could be described as nothing else. She stiffly patted her charge's back one last time before more or less pushing her upright.

The sniffling woman was indeed the bride. She was shorter than she had looked in the photograph with Ray, her green eyes red-rimmed from crying.

"Violet." Another hiss, directed at me. Nathaniel took a step away from the tense little group, motioning me closer to him.

"What's going on?" I whispered as soon as I was close enough. "Why is she crying?"

He shook his head. "Her dress wasn't shipped. Or it wasn't shipped on time."

"Because no one here seems to be able to follow simple directions." The voice that cut through the clamor was edged with ice. I turned, expecting Emeline. But it was the other woman who had spoken.

"Mrs. Brant—" Nathaniel began.

"It was a simple enough task," Emeline's mother snapped. "But apparently it was a bit too challenging for you, Nathaniel."

"Yes, and now everything is ruined." That came from Emeline, who dissolved into tears again. One of her bridesmaids, a short young woman with dark skin and long black hair in dozens of tiny braids, stepped forward to wrap an arm around her. She was, I noticed, one of the two who had been standing aside earlier, while Emeline cried in her mother's arms.

"I assure you," Nathaniel said, drawing himself up, "everything is not ruined. We'll have the dress, or I'll work a miracle, but either way, Emeline, you will walk down that aisle a vision in white. Now." He clapped his hands sharply. "Violet, my assistant, will take the bridesmaids to their villas, and Emeline and her mother will come with me. There's dinner to get ready for, after all."

Emeline's mother shot Nathaniel a glare that could have scorched the paint off a Mercedes. "There clearly aren't enough of you people to handle this many bridesmaids."

"Nonsense," Nathaniel answered breezily, already shooing the girls in the direction of the terminal doors. "They're women. Not farm animals. One assistant should be quite capable of getting them where they need to go."

It was, in fact, going to take two carts to get the bridesmaids all transported, but I wasn't keen to step into the middle of Nathaniel and Mrs. Brant's staring contest to point that out. Andi and I could handle that issue between the two of us.

"So. Ladies," I said, moving toward the terminal doors as fast as I could while still attempting to look professional. Nathaniel had definitely just poked the bear. No way I was sticking around to watch the aftermath of that. "Shall we?"

Before anyone could change their minds—although I was pretty sure none of *them* wanted to be around the mother of the bride right now either—I had them divided between my cart and Andi's. A couple of island employees made swift work of their luggage, and I silently thanked them for being so prompt. All I wanted was to have my foot on the gas pedal of the cart and get these girls to their villas.

The girl who'd comforted Emeline slid into the front seat beside me, braids swinging around her shoulders. I gave her a little smile, which she returned, though it didn't quite reach her eyes. She seemed frustrated, either with the bride or with the whole situation.

"I'm Shannon," she offered as I started up the cart.

Shannon, I recalled, was the name of the maid of honor. Which meant she was presumably the bride's best friend. Although she hadn't quite acted like it back in the terminal, at least not until Emeline's mother got out of the way, and I wondered what kinds of dynamics were really at play there.

"Violet," I answered.

In the back seat the other girls were chattering about the flowers and speculating on what their villas would be like.

"I think you should know," Shannon said, "that Emma isn't usually like that. It's been a long couple of weeks, and the dress was kind of the last straw."

It seemed like a reasonable explanation, but I remembered Nathaniel cautioning that the bride was high-strung.

"Any bride would be upset to find out her wedding dress was in danger of not arriving on time," I finally said, deciding on a diplomatic answer.

Shannon looked out at the scenery rolling past and didn't say anything more.

We arrived at the bridal villa a few minutes later, the carts emptying quickly as the bridesmaids spilled out, exclaiming at the elegant building.

"This way, ladies," Andi said briskly. "Your guest villas are in the main building where Emeline will be staying."

They followed as she led them along the footpath that circled the bridal suite, named the Villa of Bliss. I couldn't quite suppress an eye roll at the name. I'm sure it was apt in most cases, in a place like this, but in the moment it struck me as highly ironic. I hoped that after the wayward dress appeared and the bride had a nap, her life would return to a state more suited to the name of her villa. And certainly both she and Ray would be in a blissful state after the wedding. Or would they?

The rumble of a cart announced the arrival of Nathaniel, with a stiff-backed Mrs. Brant riding shotgun and a dejected-looking Emeline huddled in the back seat, clutching a handkerchief.

Seeing her like this, miserable when she should be radiant and glowing, my heart actually went out to the girl. Maybe the mother was just that domineering, or maybe the farewell lunch at her job had been more emotional than she'd expected. Or she was just exhausted and stressed over the missing dress. But no bride should start the home stretch to her wedding day in tears. I stepped up to the cart as Nathaniel pulled to a stop.

"Here we are," he said, cheery as though the bride wasn't a breath away from crying again. "This is Emeline's villa. Vivien, you're right there. First across the path."

Mrs. Brant—Vivien—stepped down from the cart, shot one disdainful glance at Nathaniel, and strode off to her villa, leaving her sodden daughter in the cart to apparently fend for herself. I scowled after the retreating, ramrod-straight back. Then I turned to Emeline, putting on a smile and holding out a hand to help her from the cart.

I'm not sure what I had expected, but I was totally thrown off guard by the woman who turned to me. Gone were the drooping shoulders and the downcast eyes, and in their place was a steely determination. She stepped from the cart without taking my hand.

"I need my dress," she said, not sharp but steady. "Here with me. As soon as you can make it happen."

And with that Emeline turned on her heel and went up the steps of the villa.

I stood, staring at the closed door. I'd dealt with bad customers in the past, but who hadn't been bad, exactly. She'd just switched gears so quickly. While I was still trying to process what had just happened, Nathaniel lay a hand on my arm.

"You need to find that dress and get it here. No matter the cost." He held out a printed sheet of paper. "The name of the shipping company is on here, along with a tracking number. Call them. Now. Get this resolved."

He climbed into his cart and started the engine, executing a ponderous turn and starting down the path. I scanned the paper in my hand and sighed. Time to see if I could work miracles.

Chapter Four

After twenty minutes on the phone with the shipping company, things seemed to be resolved. The dress would be on a charter flight to the island, scheduled to arrive the following afternoon. I breathed a sigh of relief, hoped it wasn't premature, and went to find Nathaniel. He was up at the main villa, supervising the seating arrangements for the dinner. The look he gave me when I showed up was a little desperate.

"I don't want to see your face unless you have good news," he said as he straightened up from a place setting and crossed the room to where I was standing.

I gave him my best smile. "The dress has been located and will be on a charter flight, leaving New York bright and early, and will arrive tomorrow in the early afternoon. I have the shipping company's solemn promise."

Nathaniel drew a deep breath and let it out again, a smile crossing his face.

"Fantastic. Now. Walk with me a minute." He headed down the villa steps to where the carts were parked and dropped his notebook on the front seat. When he turned to me, his smile was gone. "I hear you allowed the groom to drive you around in one of the carts."

Oh, of course. "He wanted to drive it," I answered. "What was I supposed to do? Tell him no?"

Nathaniel sighed, raising a hand to rub at the bridge of his nose. "No. No you are not. But in the future please at least attempt to subtly dissuade him, hmm? He's not your driver, Violet. You're his. You need to practice being unobtrusive. Couples don't want the wedding planner's assistant constantly underfoot."

I bit my lip. He was right. I was here to help prepare a wedding, not flirt with the groom. Which was, I had to admit to myself, what I'd been doing.

I looked past his shoulder at the lush tropical backdrop: the blue sky, the birds flitting through the trees. It was all so beautiful, and as much as I wanted to explain myself I simply nodded instead. This wasn't a conversation I really should have with Nathaniel, and the less said right now the better. I was afraid he'd send me packing, and I didn't want to leave this little slice of paradise a minute sooner than I had to.

"Good. Then go wait for the groomsmen at the terminal. They should be fairly pleasant, although it's likely they've started the celebration early. But you won't have any trouble getting them situated."

He stepped up into his cart and I sighed and hopped into my own, watching him maneuver away. He hadn't quite seemed to get the hang of driving the things yet; his cart veered from side to side on the narrow path. I wondered how boisterous this group was going to be, and just what Nathaniel meant by "unobtrusive". Maybe they'd be so wrapped up in themselves I wouldn't be noticed.

But that wasn't the case. I could hear shouts and laughter through the open doors as I pulled up to the terminal. At least they sounded happy. Andi and several of the island employees emerged from the building, carrying luggage.

"Hey. How's it going?"

She carefully arranged the bags in her cart before turning to me, her face as impassive as ever. Did she go to some kind of school to learn to do that? I'd need to ask at some point. Learning to keep a straight face around Nathaniel and his—our—clients might be useful.

Then she broke into a wide grin. "You'll like them. They're far better company than the bride. Or her mother." She shook her head. "Not that I'm speaking ill of the guests, you understand. But I'm equal parts glad she's your responsibility rather than mine, and sorry she's your load to bear."

I laughed. "It's okay. It's part of the job, I guess. Not every guest or client is going to be a ray of sunshine. The groom is fine, and most of the bridesmaids seem okay. Honestly, the bride might just be under a lot of stress."

Andi gave me a knowing look. "If you can take four this time, I'll take three."

"Sure."

She turned and opened the door again and the noise level, which had dimmed somewhat, rose considerably. I hesitated, and she pushed me gently through the door.

"Go get 'em, tiger." The impassive look was back, but there was a glint in her eye.

"Hey, guys." Nothing. The laughter continued, the guys ignoring me completely.

I pulled out my diner voice, the one I'd used to call orders back to the kitchen when I was waitressing to pay for school. "Gentlemen! If I can have your attention!" It wasn't the most dignified sound, but it worked.

There was a startling beat of silence as everyone turned to look at me. And then there were seven very happy-looking guys smiling my way. I returned the smiles, scanning the crowd for the ringleader. There's always one. I zeroed in on him: tall, lanky, his dark hair shaved short on the sides and left longer on top. There were a few visible tattoos and I caught the flash of silver from an ear piercing or two.

"Hi, I'm Violet." I extended my hand toward him and he took it, a smile on his face.

"Hey. I'm James. Nice to meet you."

The group gathered around us and he introduced them to me in turn. They were all college friends of Ray's, from Yale. They'd all apparently taken advantage of the free Champagne on the charter flight, and quite possibly something else before the flight. At any rate, they were all in a very good mood. I herded them outside and they divided between the carts without too much more prodding from Andi or me.

James climbed in beside me and I pulled away from the terminal, Andi following with her load of groomsmen. I could hear them behind us, their shouts and calls growing fainter, muffled by the foliage as we wound our way through the jungle.

"You all seem like a very close bunch."

James leaned toward me and nodded. "It seems like we've known each other forever, honestly. But, like I told you during introductions, we actually only met freshman year of college." He laughed. "Ray's like the older brother we never had."

I turned away from the view ahead just long enough to raise an eyebrow at him. "But you're all the same age?"

"Yeah, just about."

"Though some of us are a bit more mature than others!" One of the guys in the back shouted, and there was a brief pause in the conversation while James turned around to give him the finger.

He faced forward again and grinned at me like the Cheshire cat, his eyes a blazing blue. "Have you met Ray yet?"

I nodded. "Yeah, I met him earlier today."

"He's a great guy, right?" He didn't wait for my answer. "Always looking out for you. He's one of the most loyal friends a guy could ask for."

I thought about Ray's smile. How excited he'd been to drive the golf cart. And he'd been kind to me, even though I was only the wedding planner's assistant.

"We've been waiting for this day for a long time, you know. We all knew his wedding would be an elaborate ordeal here on the island, no holds barred, no expense spared." His hand was on my arm and I turned to him. His look was intense.

"Wait, that sounds terrible." James paused. "I just mean we knew that when Ray finally got hitched it would be a time to remember."

"I bet," I replied, glancing at him. "So, you're the best man?"

James laughed, relaxing back in his seat. "That I am. Or at least that best one for the job."

His laughter was contagious and I found myself smiling. Ray and his friends seemed a lot more relaxed than the mercurial Emeline and her bridesmaids. This group was cheerful and easy-going, clearly looking forward to having a good time. But then, weddings always were more of the bride's worry than the groom's.

"So I understand there's a bachelor party planned for us tonight? A send-off for Ray, before his life with the ball and chain begins?" The teasing tone I'd expected with that statement was completely missing. He caught my glance and shrugged.

"She's not my first choice for Ray, to be honest." The smile and the jovial attitude were gone. "She's probably the only thing we haven't agreed on. It's something we don't even talk about anymore. Or Ray doesn't. I've tried to tell him she's not right for him, but he's got some misguided sense of duty or loyalty or something when it comes to Emeline. And the pressure from his family doesn't help."

I blinked in the bright sunshine, not sure what to say to this, or if I should say anything at all. Did everyone share this much information with wedding planners? Nathaniel hadn't said much about this, and I was sure his idea of me being inconspicuous didn't include inspiring anti-Emeline confessions from the best man.

"Sorry if that sounds harsh. This is old news to us; we've been trying to talk sense into Ray since he proposed to her."

"But you're all here. To be part of his wedding." I had the sudden disturbing image of all the groomsmen speaking up in unison when the minister asked if there were any objections to the marriage. My alarm was either evident in my voice or on my face, because James broke into a wide grin.

"We're here for Ray, yeah," one of the other guys said.

"He thinks he's doing the right thing. I'll give one last try at talking sense into him, but after that..." James shrugged again. "I won't stand in his way on the big day." I pulled up in front of Ray's villa. Almost immediately after I heard the sound of Andi's cart pulling up behind me, and then the whoops and shouts as the guys all climbed out. Ray came down the villa steps and was instantly engulfed by his friends. James turned to me and placed his hand on my shoulder.

"Thanks for the ride, Violet. And listen, please don't think we're all a bunch of selfish jerks who are just upset we're losing our best friend to marriage, because that really isn't the truth." He watched Ray for a moment, laughing with his friends amongst backslapping and handshakes. His voice grew low and serious as he went on.

"We don't even hate Emeline. She's just not the right girl for Ray, and he shouldn't be marrying for— Well, I guess things are different when you're richer than Croesus. But he's not going to be happy with her. We all know it. He's just still got to see that for himself, I guess."

Ray broke away from the group, walking down the villa steps toward my cart. "Hey, James," he called as he got closer. "Flirting with the prettiest girls as always I see, and no time for your best friend." He pulled James out of the cart, embracing him tightly.

My cheeks grew flushed. There was a moment when our eyes met and my heart did a funny little flip-flop. I took a deep breath, hoping I didn't look as flustered as I felt. Me having meaningful eye contact with someone else's future husband, who was also technically my client, was not something Nathaniel would approve of.

And then, as though he'd heard the thought, Nathaniel's voice was in my ear, loud and clear, jerking me upright and sending my heart thudding in a different direction.

"Where are you?"

"I'm at Ray's... the groom's villa. I just dropped off the—"

"Then I need you back at the terminal. Ray's parents are here and I have them. But the grandparents are waiting. For *you*. Get there and get them to their villa."

Chapter Five

"Trouble in paradise?"

I jerked my head up. Ray was standing next to the cart, watching me. James had disappeared into the villa.

"Nothing at all. Everything's just fine." I pasted a professional smile on my face and reached for the key on the dashboard. I heard his laugh as I fumbled, and failed, to start the cart.

"Don't take this the wrong way, Violet, but you're a terrible liar."

I gave up trying to start the cart or keep up the facade that everything was fine. I sat back in the seat, blowing out a sigh. "Your grandparents are here and I'm late getting them to their villa. Nathaniel is already stressed, and getting a bit touchy."

That was, in retrospect, probably not something I should have said to the man who'd hired my boss.

"That's not so bad," Ray said. "At least it's not the dress. Again."

I winced. "You heard?"

"Yeah. And I'm sure it wasn't pretty. Emeline picked that dress out before anything else. Maybe before I even proposed. But it's her wedding day. She should have what she wants." He sighed. "And all she wants is that dress."

He rested one hand on the frame of the cart and leaned in toward me. I caught a whiff of scent. His cologne, rich and spicy, but subtle. And underneath that was clean, sun-warmed skin. Just Ray. I inhaled, barely resisting the overwhelming urge to close my eyes and lean over to draw a deeper breath. But then he was talking and I forced myself to focus on the words and not how wonderful he smelled.

"Don't worry about my grandparents. You'll like them. Grandpa Andrew and Bartholomew are probably just happy to have some time together, telling stories and making up new ones, with my grandmother as an adoring audience of one. My parents..." Ray shrugged again. "They might be a little more of a challenge. Mom's pretty much a stickler for being on time and on schedule, but Nathaniel can handle her I'm sure."

"I hope so. It seems like I'm always one step behind today." I shook my head. "Hopefully once Emeline's settled and the dress arrives..." My voice trailed off. "But this isn't about me. It's your wedding. I shouldn't be complaining." *To my client, of all people.* "I'm sorry, Ray."

"Don't be. I don't mind listening." A smile played over his lips. "And I think everyone, including you, should be enjoying themselves. This is a beautiful island. Kind of magical, honestly. I know you're here to do a job, but you should try to relax and make some time to just take it all in." He put his hand on my shoulder and I stopped breathing, afraid to move for fear he'd pull away. His touch felt electrifying, as if my skin were on fire.

"Promise me you'll let me know if things get overwhelming, okay?" His voice was sincere, and I managed to nod my head. He straightened, giving my shoulder a tight squeeze before removing his grip.

I reluctantly started the cart and Ray took a step back. "I'll let you get back to work."

I nodded. "Enjoy your afternoon with the guys, and your dinner. I'll see you tomorrow."

"You won't be there tonight?"

As much as I tried not to notice, and as much I tried to tell myself it was all my imagination, Ray's smile dimmed just a little. There was no sense in thinking he was going to miss me at dinner. This was his wedding, after all, not a date. But my heart still did a little flutter in my chest.

"No, not tonight. You'll be in the capable hands of Bartholomew's staff for the dinner."

"Well, then, thanks for all your help today, with the guys and getting them here in one piece. They can be quite a handful." He glanced at the villa. "Speaking of them, I'd better make sure they're not tearing the place apart."

"They seem like a great bunch of guys, especially James."

Ray's smile returned and he looked at me with a raised eyebrow. "I see James has worked his charm on you, then." Then his expression grew serious. "But, yeah, they are pretty great. I honestly can't imagine my life without them in it, as crazy as they can get. This wouldn't be the same without them here."

Like he'd been summoned James appeared, standing on the wide porch and waving a bottle of beer in Ray's direction.

"And so it begins," Ray said with a short laugh. He gave me one last smile before he turned and walked up the steps, taking the beer from James. They watched me execute a not so bad turn-around, and I gave them a wave before heading off down the path to the terminal.

More than anything now I wanted some alone time in my own little corner of paradise, but Ray's grandparents were my responsibility. And after Ray's reassurances, maybe it wouldn't be so bad. Then I remembered I was working for Nathaniel. Whatever the guests thought didn't matter; it was all about what Nathaniel thought. And my own little corner of paradise seemed further away.

I'd splurged on a new swimsuit, the first one I'd owned in years, and I'd been thinking about taking my first dip in this amazingly blue ocean. Trips to the beach were few and far between when I was growing up, and they had never been to any beaches like the one outside my room. And I hadn't ever really been hugely fond of the water. But then, I'd never been in any water like the water here.

Still, work had to come first. I headed back to the terminal, arriving just in time to see Nathaniel pulling away with Ray's parents. I wasn't sure what I expected but they were dressed far more formally than anyone, save Mrs. Brant. As I climbed out of my cart, I watched Nathaniel ferrying them down the path toward their villa, his cart traveling at a sedate pace.

I sighed and turned toward the glass doors of the terminal and thought about families, how sometimes all the members are so much alike in looks and mannerisms you can pick them out of a crowd. And here, how Ray's parents looked so uptight and starchily stiff, and yet Ray was so relaxed and easy-going.

It seemed, as I pulled open the door and was greeted with peals of laughter, that his genes had come from a little farther up the tree. Standing in the center of the room was Bartholomew, hands on his hips, watching a tall, white-haired man in the midst of them waving his arms over his head, apparently in the middle of an animated recitation. A small silver-haired woman was seat at his side, laughing up at them both. As I watched, Bartholomew put his hands on his knees and surrendered to wave after wave of laughter.

Not wanting to interrupt, I hesitated just inside the door. A moment later Bartholomew straightened, and he caught my eye. With a wide smile he hurried across the room, pulling me into the small group.

"Violet, my dear. Come here. Meet my old friend, Nathan Carter, and his lovely wife, Ione. Violet is one half of the wedding planning team working with Emeline and Ray."

The woman rose, extending her hand. I hesitated in reaching out to shake it, fearful of hurting her. She looked so dainty. But I almost winced at the strength of her hand gripping mine.

"Violet, lovely to meet you. This is my husband, Drew. You're working with Nathaniel, then? How exciting... traveling about to all these exotic locations. Such a romantic job."

Andrew Carter had come to stand beside his wife. He towered over both of us and I could see the family resemblance. Ray's same strong jaw and straight nose. The only difference, aside from several decades, was the thick shock of snowy hair.

"Nice to meet you, young lady." He shook my hand much more gently than his wife had, and graced me with the same warm smile Ray had. I instantly liked the man.

"And now that you're in good hands," Drew said, leaning down and kissing Ione full on the lips, "I'm off."

An instant later he was out the doors. I watched him for a moment, expecting him to climb into the cart, but he strode off down one of the paths. I turned to Ione.

"He isn't walking, is he?" It was hot and humid and I was already wilting, just from riding in the cart. Then again, he was wearing a light linen shirt and I was still corseted in my jacket.

"Don't look so alarmed, dear." She took my arm, leading me out the doors into the bright sunshine. "He walks everywhere, you know. And he knows his way around this island. He'll be fine."

"Well, okay. If you think…"

"I don't think. I know." Her gentle laugh carried on the breeze. "I've been married to the man for almost sixty years."

I had no choice but to smile. She was utterly charming. Andi had joined us, loading their luggage into the back of her cart. I heard a brief conversation between them and saw Ione pat her arm. Andi gave the older woman one of her rare smiles before disappearing back into the terminal. It occurred to me they must be frequent visitors here, Andi and the rest of the staff almost like family.

Ione turned, her bright blue eyes fixed on me. "I, however, have no intention of walking. Shall we?" She climbed into the cart and I joined her. As charming as she was, I sensed a core of steel.

"We shall." I started the cart and headed down the path toward her villa, keeping an eye out for Drew in any kind of distress along the way. But I didn't come across him lying prostrate on any of the paths. We also didn't pass him along the way, which puzzled me. Maybe there were other paths not meant for the carts. Or maybe he just knew his way through the jungle. Somehow, I wouldn't put it past him.

"You must be very excited for Ray and Emeline," I said, turning to Ione.

There was a longer pause than I would have expected. I glanced at Ione and saw the same look I'd seen from Ray, the smile on her face not quite reaching her eyes.

"Ray is happy, and that's what's important." She drew a deep breath and turned to me. "Have you met Emeline?"

"Yes." I wondered if this was going to be a repeat of the conversation I'd had with James.

"My grandson is a pretty amazing young man. But he suffers from something I call 'white knight syndrome.'"

I shook my head. "I'm not sure what you mean."

"Ray feels the need to rescue women. Specifically Emeline. He has it in his head that he's going to make her happy, despite the whole relationship being more about their parents than either of them."

"I see." I didn't, really, but I wasn't going to admit that to Ione. At least not yet. I wasn't sure what Emeline might need rescuing from, unless it was her mother.

"You see, Emeline has had a rather... unfortunate life up to this point. Her father died when she was quite young, and her mother is a bit... overbearing. Have you met Mrs. Brant?"

"I have, yes."

"Well, when Ray first met Emeline, through a charity Emeline volunteered for and Ray contributed a great deal to, one that Mrs. Brant was also involved in, it became clear to Ray that Emeline was terribly unhappy. He might have stuck to other methods of trying to help her, but then the whole company merger issue came into it and I suppose he decided that he was going to be the one to make her happy. Then, I think, he convinced himself he was the only one who could."

I bit my lip, unsure if I was required to provide some reply. But Ione went on in the face of my confused silence.

"While the former might be possible, the latter certainly isn't true. And the only person he's going to definitely make happy is Vivien." Ione leaned toward me, a hand on my forearm. "You're familiar with the term 'gold-digger,' aren't you?"

I almost drove off the path. If wedding planning frequently involved families and friends divulging their innermost thoughts about the opposite family, I might have to think about adding a psychology degree to my little hospitality degree. I'd learned about budgets and market strategies, but nothing about family dynamics as they related to soon-to-be married couples. I wondered if Nathaniel was going through the same thing with Emeline and Mrs. Brant. It chilled me to the bone to think of explaining all this to Nathaniel. I was pretty sure having the grandmother of the groom telling me her future granddaughter-in-law was a gold-digger was not what Nathaniel meant by remaining unobtrusive.

"You think Emeline is one?" I blurted.

"What? Oh no, dear. I think Vivien is. She wants her family to return to the grandeur it once had." Ione shook her head. "But the best way to pan for gold at her age is with a daughter."

"But Ray is happy, right?" I asked, nerves bubbling in my stomach. "I mean, he loves Emeline?"

"He's in love with the idea of rescuing the girl. But that's not true love." Ione sighed. "He's caught up in duty and honor, things his parents have told him are important."

We'd finally arrived at Ione's villa. I parked the cart and turned off the motor. She turned to me, her eyes bright.

"When I first saw Drew, I knew right then that he was the man I wanted to spend the rest of my life with. He felt the same. We were inseparable from the beginning. And we were married three months after we met."

"Love at first sight..." I smiled, imagining them all those years ago, young and hopelessly in love.

"Yes. Exactly. Drew and I followed our hearts and never looked back." Ione tapped her head with her index finger. "Ray is following his head. I don't think he trusts his heart." She made that noise that only grandmothers can make, somewhere between a *tsk* and a *tut*; mildly disapproving, but still full of love.

"But what do I know? I'm just a silly old woman." Ione drew a deep breath, giving me a bright smile. She turned, looking behind us down the path. "And here comes the traveler, back from wherever he's been."

I looked behind us and there was Drew, striding up the path, looking just as fresh as when he had stepped out of the terminal. He stopped beside the cart, holding out his arm to Ione.

"Ione, my love, would you like an escort to our villa?"

Ione smiled up at Drew, looking positively girlish. She took his arm, stepping gracefully out of the cart. Then she turned back to me. "Thank you, Violet. For the ride and the chat. It was kind of you to indulge me. Although you were rather a captive audience."

And with that, she and Drew went up the steps to their villa. I watched them, arm in arm, and then Drew opened the door and held it for Ione. Just before she stepped through she turned, caught my eye, and gave me a wave.

I turned the cart around and tapped my mic. "Nathaniel? I've dropped off the grandparents. Where do you want me next?"

There was silence. I tapped the mic again. "Nathaniel? Are you there?"

"Of course I'm here." Even through the microphone, I could sense the tension.

"Okay. What do you want me to do next?"

There was a pause, as though he was thumbing through that leather notebook of his. Then, "I need you to go up to the main villa and check on the flowers. They should have come in this afternoon, and they'll be in refrigeration. I want to make certain they're correct. You have the flower list?"

I reached for the packet I'd tucked under the seat and glanced through it. "I do."

"Good. Go make sure no one has screwed up anything else."

THE FLOWERS, THANKFULLY, were doing just fine. Which was a relief. I wasn't sure I could have handled another major setback after the rest of the day. Something going right for once was exactly what I needed. As I stepped out of the building and into the late-afternoon sun, however, I nearly ran directly into Emeline.

She took a step back, as startled as I was, and for an instant we stared at each other. At least, I thought she didn't look like she'd been crying recently. She'd also changed clothes, and was wearing a light summer dress of pale green linen. She looked a lot more comfortable than I felt. And, unlike that afternoon, she was impeccably made up, not a hair out of place.

"Miss Brant," I said. "Excuse me. Is there anything I can do for you?"

"No." She gave me a considering sort of once-over, like it was the first time she was really seeing me.

I was a good deal shorter than she was, and my build tended more toward hourglass than wood nymph. The skirt suit and its polyester jacket probably didn't help. I was sure I looked rumpled, and I self-consciously pushed a loose strand of hair back behind my ear.

"Thank you," she added. That surprised me. After the way she'd acted before, I wouldn't have expected her to direct anything more than orders at the staff.

Maybe I was being unfair, and she'd just been under a lot of stress after all. Her maid of honor had certainly seemed to think that was the case.

"Of course," I said, realizing that I hadn't answered. "Any time. We're here to help you."

She smiled. It wasn't quite the dazzling expression from the engagement photo, but there was something sweet in it that made me warm to her. "And I'm sure you're doing a fabulous job," she said. "Speaking of, did you hear anything about the dress?"

"It will be here tomorrow."

"Perfect. Thank you."

And with that she was gone, leaving me staring after her for the second time that day. She seemed better. But she didn't, I thought as I watched her disappear through the glass doors, seem like a woman about to get married to the love of her life. I wondered just what it was that James and Ione had been hinting at. Did either member of the soon-to-be-married couple even *want* the wedding they were about to share?

Chapter Six

I called Nathaniel again as I turned away from the main villa and my questions about Emeline and Ray, anticipating another task. Instead, after reassuring him that the flowers were fine, I heard the words I'd been anticipating all day. "You're free for the rest of the night."

I tried to keep the joy and relief out of my voice. "Are you sure? It's still early..."

"I'm sure. The family dinner tonight is taken care of and I want you well rested for tomorrow. The rest of the guests will be arriving and I want them transported with a little more speed and efficiency than you showed today. Do I make myself clear?"

"Yes, Nathaniel."

"And I want that dress to be your priority. First thing in the morning, call the shipping company."

There was a burst of static and the rest of Nathaniel's comments were lost. I nodded anyway. There was no mistaking what my priority for tomorrow would be.

But for now, I was free. And that meant freeing myself from this polyester nightmare of a jacket and taking a swim in that beautiful blue ocean waiting for me outside my room. I'd skipped lunch, and breakfast was a long-forgotten memory, but food could wait. The ocean beckoned, and for the first time that day I had my cart at top speed on the way back to my room.

Excitement aside, I did remember to plug the cart in the way Andi had showed me before I ran up the steps to my room. My luggage was still just inside the door, and I dug through, finding the swimsuit at the bottom. The hateful jacket—along with the rest of my clothes—ended up on the floor.

The sand was warm beneath my feet and I stopped at the water's edge, looking out at the ocean, mesmerized by the view. The sun was low in the sky, a few clouds sprawled across the horizon, and the light had changed. It wasn't the brilliant glow from earlier. Now it was tinged with yellow and orange, the water a deeper, glowing shade of blue beneath its radiance.

Who knew three simple things—sand, water, and sunlight—could come together in such a magical way? I waded out into the water, amazed at the warmth, at how buoyant I felt. I dove into the crystal-clear water, watching the sandy bottom for shells or fish. When I surfaced I stood, the water lapping around my waist. It was heaven, no doubt about it.

I played in the water until I realized the sun had almost set, floating on my back with the changing sky above me. It was getting dark, and it occurred to me that being secluded in paradise was one thing. Being swept out to sea with no one the wiser was another. A shiver ran through me, then, as I looked out across the ocean. Against the endless stretch of it I felt very tiny, and very alone, and suddenly I wanted the security of my little room.

I discovered an incredibly soft robe in the bathroom, and what looked like dozens of fluffy white towels. For being so small, my room certainly didn't seem to be lacking any creature comforts. I snuggled into the robe, cinching the belt around my waist, and luxuriated in the cozy warmth of it until my grumbling stomach reminded me that I was starving.

But getting dressed and driving all the way to who-knows-where for food wasn't very appealing. I wasn't even sure where I was supposed to go for meals. I blew out a sigh, turning in a slow circle as though something in the room might inspire me. As I turned, I spotted a curtained alcove tucked discretely into a corner. I pulled back the curtain and grinned.

There was a small kitchen, complete with a miniature refrigerator and tiny cook top. The alcove also contained a well-stocked liquor cabinet and an assortment of cheeses and breads, all fresh and smelling wonderful. I'd totally missed seeing it before. The view from the French doors had taken all my attention. And in my haste to hit the beach, I'd also missed the welcome basket of fruit that someone—Andi probably—had left on the bedside table.

Between the fruit, bread and cheese, along with a drink, I was set with dinner. No need to change or go anywhere. I could just relax. I did a little dance around my tiny kitchen and then got busy slicing cheese and bread, and poured a glass of white wine. It took me a minute to get the cork out of the bottle and I giggled. The only wine we'd ever had at home, or that I could afford, came in bottles with a screw top. I suddenly felt awkward as I wrestled the cork out of the bottle.

I stepped out on to the back patio and stopped dead in my tracks. I'd never seen anything like the display going on over my head. The sun was just below the horizon, but the sky was brilliantly colored in yellows and purples. The undersides of the clouds were streaked in every shade of orange imaginable.

The only sounds were the soft wash of the waves on the sand and a few birds in the bushes around my room. Other than that, it was completely silent. I sat on the steps in my robe and spread my impromptu dinner beside me. The sky was growing progressively darker as I ate; the colors deepened, and finally all melded into a deep blue. I couldn't tell where the water ended and the sky began.

I nibbled on a piece of cheese, something complex and pungent, and took a sip of wine. It was cool and crisp, perfect with the cheese. I closed my eyes, sighing deeply, my muscles relaxing. I hadn't realized just how tense I was until that moment.

Abruptly, a wave of homesickness washed over me. Everyone on the island—Emeline and Ray, Ione and Drew, even Bartholomew—was with family and good friends, people they loved and cared for. And I was alone. I missed my roommate, Lydia, and my cat, Irving. I set down the food and pulled my cell phone from my purse to dial home.

Lydia answered. I was so happy to hear her voice that I almost cried.

"Violet?"

"Lydia," I answered, my voice tight with suppressed tears.

Her tone immediately switched to concern. "Are you okay? You sound upset."

"Yeah. I'm fine." I sniffled a little. "I just... I got a little homesick. I miss you guys."

"We miss you, too." Her voice was gentle. "Irving says hi. But, hon, what are you doing getting homesick in paradise?" The familiar throaty laughter pulled a smile from me. "I mean, it must be rough out there. You know it's below freezing here? And I have to walk to work in the morning."

"Yeah. I know. Sorry. I'm in paradise and I'm complaining. It's just been a really busy day and I'm finally getting to relax and... I realized how alone I was here."

"I thought you were in the middle of planning the biggest wedding in the city's history."

I sank back down on the steps. "Not right now. I'm done for the day. There's a big family dinner at the main villa, but the island staff is taking care of that."

"I don't know about you, but I'd kill for a little alone time on a tropical island. But I'd kill for any time on a tropical island. How are the lifestyles of the rich and the famous?"

"Honestly, the island is amazing. Everything you'd imagine a tropical paradise would be. The owner, Bartholomew? He's a little eccentric, but a good guy."

"What about the bride? Is she as pretty as she looked in the photographs?"

"Definitely," I said. "Not quite as tall as she looked. But definitely as pretty."

"And?" Lydia wanted details, and lots of them. But I didn't know that I should tell her what had happened with the wedding dress and Emeline's tears. Now that I'd run into her outside her mother's influence, I felt like she couldn't really be blamed for having a bit of a breakdown. Maybe I'd tell Lydia after the wedding.

"And that's really all I can tell you."

"Aw, really?"

"The rest later. I promise."

"Fine." She sighed, very long-suffering. "Are there any available groomsmen, then? Are they cute? What about the groom?"

I grinned, remembering James and the rowdy groomsmen. "They're a bunch of old friends of Ray's, all ready to have a good time. The one I spent time talking to seemed nice."

"And? Any sparks?"

Lydia had run through every single guy she knew in the tristate area, including every available cousin she had. And there had been many.

"I spent, like, ten minutes with them, and not even all of them. Besides, I'm here to work, not to find a boyfriend."

There was another sigh on the other end of the line. "Violet..."

"I'm not hiding, Lydia." It was an old argument. "This just isn't the right time or place."

"Maybe not. But it seems like no time or place is. You never look any more, Violet. Ever."

Lydia was right, as much as I hated to admit it. My last relationship hadn't been a good one.

"I'm not going to start looking for a boyfriend at some stranger's wedding, Lydia. I'm here—"

"Yeah, I know. To work." There was a weighted pause. "You haven't mentioned him yet."

"Who?" But I knew exactly *who* she meant.

"The groom. Who else? Did you meet him? Is he nice? Is he as good-looking as his pictures?"

There was a curious fizzy feeling in my chest, like I'd swallowed a mouthful of bubbles. I took a sip of wine, which made me cough and sputter.

"Violet? Did I lose you?"

"No. Just... swallowed my wine wrong. How was work?"

There was another beat of silence. "Oh, Violet. You've got it bad."

"Don't be ridiculous, Lydia." My cheeks were warm and I tried to tell myself it was from the wine. There was a noise on the other line from Lydia, a sound that usually meant she was going to call bullshit on whatever I said.

"He's really nice, sure. And handsome... and nice." I sighed. "Yeah, he's totally perfect. And yeah, I've probably got a little crush going. But the day after tomorrow he's going to be someone else's husband. And I've met her. And she's gorgeous."

I didn't—couldn't—tell Lydia about the things James and Ione had said. Couldn't tell her that at first I'd thought Emeline Brant was a spoiled brat. Whatever my feelings about her, I wasn't going to be the kind of person who stole another woman's husband from her.

"No. I know. I didn't plan this. He's just... there's something about him that's so genuine."

The last place I wanted this conversation to go was what I thought about Ray and Emeline, or that little voice that said there was something not quite right between them. Lydia would tell me point blank that it was just wishful thinking, and maybe it was.

"Listen, Lydia. I'm exhausted. And I need to be up at the crack of dawn, dealing with the missing wedding dress. I'll call you tomorrow, okay?"

We said our goodbyes and I went back inside, pouring myself another glass of wine. I wasn't actually that tired, but talking with Lydia had ignited that little prickle of guilt that had been plaguing me since I first started looking at the groom with more than platonic interest. That, and I was thinking about Evan.

It had been almost a year since he left, after one final angry tirade of accusations and threats, but the memory still lingered a little too sharply for me to easily let go of it.

That night hadn't been the first time he accused me of cheating, of not loving him, of whatever else he could think of. And he'd threatened me more than once with just what he'd do if he ever actually caught me.

By then, I'd given up trying to explain anything to Evan. There had been no point to it. I'd been worn down by the constant arguing, starting to believe the things he said about me being stupid and lazy. But that night he went too far.

He'd never gotten physical with me. All his abuse had been emotional. But Irving had jumped up on my lap during the middle of yet another argument. I'd pulled the cat closer, nuzzling his soft fur.

"You love that damn cat more than you do me."

Before I could stop him he'd swept Irving, in a snarl of slashing claws and flying fur, out of my arms and off my lap. There was a flash of black and white as Irving dove under the couch and then Evan was holding his hand, blood welling from several deep scratches.

"That fucking cat has to go! Look! Look what he did!" Evan was holding his hand out toward me, kicking the couch at the same time. There was a muffled growl and hiss from beneath the furniture, which seemed to make Evan even angrier.

I hadn't been doing a particularly great job of taking care of myself in the relationship with Evan. But that didn't mean I was going to let him hurt my cat. I jumped up from the couch, standing toe to toe with Evan.

"Out. Now. I've had enough." I took a step forward and Evan took a step back.

"The damn cat—"

"No. Not the cat. Or not *just* the cat. Everything... *and* the cat. Just leave, Evan. Go."

I'd never stood up to Evan, but suddenly everything was so clear. He needed to go and I needed to be out of this relationship. I'd taken enough. And so had Irving, apparently.

"Fine. I'll get my stuff. But you're making a huge mistake, Violet." He took a step toward the bedroom, but I got there first.

"You can get your things tomorrow when I'm at work. I want you out."

He turned back to me, and for a minute I thought I'd be joining Irving under the couch. But something had changed between us, something small but vital. Evan grabbed his jacket and stomped toward the apartment door. He turned, his hand still bleeding. Some of the anger had gone out of his eyes, replaced by a stubborn pout. He looked for all the world like the bully on the playground who had just had sand kicked in his face by the playground geek. And he didn't know what to do. There was an instant where I felt sorry for him. But then he opened his mouth and that instant passed.

"You're going to regret this, Violet. No one is ever going to love you like I do... no one's even going to want you. You're going nowhere. You're lucky I even bothered. But I'm done with you. I was going to leave you anyway."

I laughed then, because I realized just how ridiculous the whole thing was. How fragile Evan was under the shell of anger. Evan's eyes went wide, the shock on his face making me laugh harder, more than a bit of hysteria around the edges.

"You're crazy, you know that?" Those were his final words. He slammed the door and was gone.

Since then, Irving had been the only man in my life. When I found it hard to make ends meet on minimum wage and tips, Lydia had finally convinced me to share an apartment. And for the most part, things went smoothly between us. But her insistence on finding me my next boyfriend was a sticking point that came up with increasing regularity.

The sun was gone outside and a crescent moon hung in the sky, impossibly slender and bright. Above that the stars were coming out, more stars than I'd ever thought possible. I slipped off my robe, took my wine, and walked out on the beach. Everything around me was dark, just the soft light from my room spilling out onto the sand, fading the closer I got to the water.

A light breeze had picked up, still warm, but with tendrils of cool air. I shivered, goose bumps suddenly rushing up my arms.

"Enjoying the view?"

I jumped, spinning around, not quite spilling my wine.

"Oh, it's you." My heart had taken on a life of its own, thudding at double speed. Ray walked into the faint light that spilled from my room. I heard his gentle, deep laugh.

"I'm sorry, Violet. Really. I wasn't sure... I didn't want to sneak up on you, but I guess I did anyway."

We were standing at the edge of the water, both of us barefoot. I shivered again as a wave washed over my toes.

"Here." He shrugged out of his sport jacket and draped it over my shoulders.

"Thanks." It was warm from his body, the scent of his cologne filling my nostrils, and I was instantly warm and flushed, my breath picking up. I took a deep breath to clear my head and ended up inhaling the wonderful scent of Ray once more. All that managed to do was speed up my heart rate. We needed some words between us.

"Is your dinner finished already? It's still early." I took a tentative sip of my wine and then realized how tipsy I felt. But I took another swallow anyway.

Ray looked off across the water. "Yeah. I guess it is."

"Something went wrong," I said, not really a question. All the warmth went out of Ray's jacket as my heart dropped. I had images of Nathaniel trying to reach me on the wireless mic, while I cavorted in the ocean and drank wine.

"Nothing to do with anything you or Nathaniel planned," Ray assured me. "That all went off without a hitch. The staff was great, too. It's just, well... Emeline is under a lot of stress. And there was..."

"Conflict?"

"Yeah. Conflict." Ray had his hands in his pockets, drawing circles in the damp sand with his toe. There was an instant where my logical, rational brain tried to stop me from speaking, but I didn't listen.

"Do you want to come sit on the steps? I have some wine." I held up my glass, the pale white wine catching the light. For a moment, it looked like I had a glass full of stars.

"I don't want to intrude," Ray said. But he turned toward my room as I did, and we walked through the sand to the patio steps.

"Here." He took my glass, his fingers brushing against mine as he did. A little thrill went up my arm and I drew in a sharp breath. "I'll get this."

What the heck was I thinking, I wondered. But Ray was already disappearing inside, and I settled down in one of the chairs. For about half a second. Then I sat bolt upright. All my clothes—bra and panties included—were still strewn across the floor. I cringed, deciding there was nothing I could do, and sat back again in my chair.

Ray came back out onto the patio and handed me my glass. He stood for a moment, looking out over the dark water. He looked tired, worry lines creasing the corners of his eyes. But then he turned to me and gave me that brilliant smile I'd seen earlier.

"This is nice. You really are at the end of the world here. Or, at least at the end of the island." He pulled the second chair out of the shadows and sat down. "It's peaceful."

We sipped our wine in comfortable silence. I wanted to give him that. The peace that he so clearly needed. But questions about the dinner itched at me, and when the quiet had stretched out between us long enough that I thought he might be ready to answer I gave voice to them.

"So, the dinner. What happened?"

Ray swirled the wine in his glass, watching it slosh against the sides. "It was fine, at first. I'd finally gotten James and the guys to understand that it wasn't a bachelor party. There wouldn't be any strippers. No one was allowed to get outrageously drunk." He laughed.

"You met James, so you know a little of what I was up against. He was all set to send me off with a huge, booze-soaked bash, so when he heard it was a formal sit-down dinner? Well, let's say there was a protest."

"Was that the conflict?"

Ray looked down at the wooden floor of the patio, his brow creased in a frown. "No. I mean, there was a lot of complaining from the guys, you know. They were a little disappointed, I guess. But they all got dressed and we headed off to the main villa, with them more or less on their best behavior. My parents were there, and Grandma Ione and Grandpa Drew."

"And Emeline and her mother."

"Yes." He nodded. "And at first it was great, sort of. The food was great, everything was beautiful. You and Nathaniel really did an amazing job."

I was shaking my head, ready to explain what I hadn't done, but Ray wasn't looking at me.

"And then Grandma said something to Emeline's mother. I have no idea what it was, but it... You know how it is sometimes, at a party or in a group, all the chatter and noise and then everyone goes quiet at the same time?"

Ray took a long swallow of wine and turned back to me. "There was this sudden silence. Like everything had just stopped. I looked up, and Mrs. Brant was glaring at Grandma. And then she threw her napkin down on her plate, stood up, and stormed out of the room."

I closed my eyes, imaging the ramrod-straight line of Vivien Brant's spine as she marched out of the villa. It said something, I thought, that Ray still referred to his future mother-in-law by her surname.

"And then," he said, "Emeline got up and followed her. She wasn't angry, honestly. She looked like she was about to cry."

"Oh, Ray. That's awful. Did you talk to her and find out what happened?" I leaned forward, despite my better judgment, wanting only to comfort him, and lay a hand on his knee. He put his over it, giving it a small squeeze before letting go. My heart went out to him. But with that touch came a renewed prickle of guilt. I shouldn't have been thinking of how my hand felt in his, or how broad his shoulders were, or how the light played on his hair. I drew my hand away, my palm warm and tingling from the contact. I needed to focus on how to help him, if there *was* any help for this situation.

"Talking to Emeline lately has been... difficult." Ray sighed. "I'm guessing she probably hasn't managed to make the best impression on you, but she's not a bad person. In the early days, she was so easy to be around. But the closer the wedding gets, the more she... I don't know if I should talk to you about this, honestly."

"My lips are sealed," I promised him, my sincerity maybe a little bit influenced by the wine I'd had. But I meant what I said. "Nothing you tell me will leave this porch."

For a moment he looked like he might not say anything even so, then he shook his head, shoulders slumping. "It seems like something is weighing on her. More and more as time goes on. I've tried to talk to her about it, but when I ask she just tells me that she's worried about the wedding."

"And you think it's more than that?"

"I don't know what to think, honestly. Her mother is, well, you've met her. And Emeline's life hasn't been easy. I don't know if Nathaniel told you any of it."

His grandmother had, but I didn't think saying so was polite. I shook my head.

"Well." Ray finished his wine, setting the glass aside. "Her father died when she was little, and her mother has never really been happy since, I think." He stared up at the sky, as though the stars might hold the words he was looking for. "She's pushed Emeline to succeed. Pushed her to do a lot of things. And I know what we're getting into with this marriage, but I thought, maybe…"

There it was, another hint at the nature of the relationship. It was starting to take a shape I thought I could trace, but I didn't want to venture a guess yet. At least not out loud. I didn't want to say something wrong.

"What about talking to Mrs. Brant?" I suggested, not sure what else to offer. "Maybe you could find out what upset her. Smooth it over."

He laughed. A sharp, mirthless sound. "Mrs. Brant is… very hard to deal with."

There. An opening, maybe, to ask what was really going on without asking outright. My stomach twisted a little with nerves, but I went for it anyway.

"It's worth it, though, isn't it? Dealing with Mrs. Brant, I mean." I took a breath and barreled on before I could think better of my question. "A little trouble with her mother shouldn't be much beside the chance to spend the rest of your life with the woman you love."

"The woman I love," Ray echoed. His voice was low, and the words were laced with pain. His head dropped forward, his face in shadow.

I set my wine glass aside and scooted to the edge of my chair. "Ray."

He looked up at me then, the soft light spilling from the windows behind us catching the glint of his eyes. I couldn't tell whether there were tears there, but they held so much sadness.

"Do you love her?" I asked, my heart racing behind my ribs.
"I do... I think." He shook his head. "I did."

Chapter Seven

There it was: the answer I'd been looking for. Hoping for. But I couldn't take any joy in it. Not when I knew how much it hurt him. Not when I knew how selfish I was to have ever wanted that answer at all.

I reached out, my hand cupping his cheek. *Why go through with it, then?* But I thought I knew what the answer was going to be, and the question seemed cruel. "I'm so sorry, Ray," I said instead. "Truly."

He caught my hand in his, and for an instant I thought he was going to push me away. But he drew a deep breath and closed his eyes, turning his cheek against my palm. A long moment passed in silence between us, and then he spoke.

"It's so easy to tell you this, Violet. Why is that? You're practically a stranger." He opened his eyes, and his gaze held mine. "But you're the one I found when things fell apart."

"Sometimes," I said, "it's easier to talk to someone who doesn't know you very well. You don't have to worry about hurting them. But... your parents, your grandparents—they're here for you. I'm sure they'd want to hear what you have to say."

He sighed again. "They love me. And my grandparents, at least, want me to be happy. I'm sure my parents do, too, but they...they think of marriage as a contract. Like a business arrangement."

"You don't have to, though. What about Ione and Drew? Love at first sight. Surely she's told you how they met?"

"I know the story. But it's not like that. Not anymore. That was in a different time." He shook his head. "This is real life, not a fairytale. My grandparents found each other when life was less complicated. It's not that simple now."

"Maybe love doesn't have to be that complicated."

His eyes met mine, surprise in them, or maybe something like longing, and I held my breath. Gently, I untangled my hand from his and tapped his forehead with my finger. "Your grandmother says you're thinking from here."

I moved my hand lower, placing my palm on his chest. "And not from here." The words came out as barely a whisper. I kept my hand where it was, feeling the heat of his body through the thin fabric of his shirt.

"Do you think that's true?" His voice was low, his eyes holding mine with a gaze that carried a great deal more passion than I'd seen before. Passion that made my heart skip a beat.

"I think you should be happy."

"It's not that easy," Ray said, resignation heavy in his tone. "But thank you for listening to me ramble anyway. You're a sweet person, Violet."

"Very sweet," a man agreed from a few feet down the beach.

The voice made us both jump. I startled back from Ray, face flaming, and turned to see James sauntering across the sand to stand at the porch railing, giving us both a look that said he knew exactly what was going on. We hadn't done anything. Not really. But that look still made my stomach churn.

"There's a storm coming," James said. "It shouldn't be too bad, but I thought you should know." He turned his eyes to Ray. "You should come back to the villa. We'll throw you a proper bachelor party, since the dinner went down in flames."

"I'll be right there," Ray said.

James stood watching us for an instant longer and then he shrugged, shooting us both a grin that might have been approval or might just have been silently communicating *'This is going to blow up in everyone's face, but have fun while it lasts, I guess,'* and went back the way he'd come.

We were both still, watching him go until he disappeared around a bend in the shoreline. When we turned back to each other, I wasn't sure what to say. Ray didn't seem sure either. Instead, he leaned forward, his arms going around my shoulders. He pulled me into a quick, awkward embrace that was probably a goodbye. I closed my eyes.

Ray drew back, or I thought he did. I turned my head just as he moved and his lips brushed against my cheek. There was a split second where I knew I could turn away, make this—whatever this was—end gracefully.

But of course, I didn't. I turned my face toward Ray and our lips met, so softly at first I thought I imagined the contact. Then that contact intensified, his lips firm against mine, moving over them until he found the perfect meeting of our mouths. I sighed and he pulled me closer, one hand reaching up to cup my cheek.

His kiss was like nothing I'd ever experienced. It was gentle and insistent, and full of something that felt like longing all at the same time. I gave up any pretense of thinking this was wrong and met him fully, my hand sliding up over his linen shirt, my fingers reading the Morse Code of his heartbeat at his throat. It was steady and strong and fast, but not nearly as fast as mine.

His fingers worked into the damp hair at the nape of my neck, holding me firmly, with no intention of letting go. His other hand slid beneath the jacket, slowly moving over my bare skin, coming to rest just above my hip, at the edge of my suit. I shifted on the chaise, our knees bumping together briefly, and then I was pressed against his chest as he pulled me closer.

The urgency in that embrace was intense and took me by surprise. Not just the intensity from Ray, but the intensity welling up inside of me. This was wrong on so many levels, but right then, in the moment, everything was perfect.

His mouth was moving over mine, his lips parted, the brush of his tongue against my closed lips warm and teasing. I parted my lips and his tongue slid against mine and I heard that little keening noise I make, deep in the back of my throat. I was melting into him at a rapid rate.

His hands tightened on my body and he pulled me up in one smooth move, pressing me hard against him. I wrapped my arms around his neck, stood on tiptoe and threw myself into the kiss, any last hesitancy gone. My hands found the soft swirls of his hair as his found their way beneath the jacket. With a careless shrug, it landed on the chaise and the touch of the breeze on my skin sent a shiver down my spine. Instantly Ray's arms were around me, the warmth of his body sending completely different sensations along my nerves.

The kiss deepened, amazingly so. I'd never been so lost in a kiss. It went on and on, neither of us able to get enough of each other. I'd stopped thinking of Ray as the groom, as Emeline's future husband. He was the man in my arms, the man making me dizzy and giddy and desperate for more.

Emeline's future husband. I broke away with a gasp, hand to my mouth.

"Oh, Ray. I-I'm not— I don't—" I stumbled out of his arms, sitting down hard when the backs of my legs hit the edge of the chaise.

"Are you okay?"

I had to give it to him. He had gone from wanting to concerned in the space of a breath, his eyebrows drawing together and his eyes soft as he sank down across from me and took my hand in his own. I shivered and thought about pulling it back, but I just couldn't make myself break the contact first.

"I'm fine. It's just..."

"That shouldn't have happened?"

I nodded. "I shouldn't have—"

Ray held up his hand. "Stop. You didn't do anything, Violet. Please don't think that."

"But you're getting married."

He looked out over the ocean again, his brow creased, but only for a moment. I saw the corner of his mouth curl into a smile.

"Yeah. I am." He turned back to me, the smile broadening. "But I won't lie to you, Violet. Kissing you, it was... I haven't felt that way in a long time."

"That doesn't make it right."

"But it *felt* right, didn't it?"

It had. It had felt more right than any kiss I'd ever shared with anyone else. That didn't chase away the knowledge that I had nearly just done the worst possible thing I could have chosen to do with a client.

He was still looking at me. Waiting.

"Yeah," I said. "Yeah. It was... good."

He held out his hands. I lay mine hesitantly in them, and he pulled me to my feet. "If it helps, I didn't come here looking for that. It's not what I was expecting."

"I know." I did. "It's not what I planned either. Or would have planned. Or..."

"Or wanted?" His tone was gently teasing, but his eyes were locked on mine.

I had no ready answer. The silence stretched between us, and Ray watched me. He knew already how much I'd wanted it. That had become more than obvious as soon as he leaned in. Had probably been plain well before that. I had never, after all, been very good at lying.

Finally, he nodded. Then, without saying anything else, he leaned forward, kissing my forehead softly. I closed my eyes and breathed in his scent for what was likely to be the last time. At least this close. It was the end of any contact beyond the most strictly professional that I was going to have with Ray, maybe the end of any contact at all. I wanted to remember the scent of his cologne and his skin, the feel of his hands, his lips on my forehead. If Nathaniel heard even a whisper of what had just happened, I'd be going home on the next charter.

Ray straightened, tipping his forehead briefly against mine. "It will be fine, Violet. Don't worry."

"I'm not worried."

The warmth of his breath, still so close, tickled my skin. I wondered if it was better or worse to draw it out this way. "You're a terrible liar," he said.

"Yeah." I pulled away. "I know. And, yeah. I'm worried."

"It really will be okay. Everything will go on like it's supposed to, and..." Ray smiled down at me. "We'll just have this little moment that we had."

"But what about Emeline?"

I wanted to take the question back as soon as her name left my lips. The smile on Ray's face faded, the light going out of his eyes, and it took a chip out of my heart.

"She doesn't need to know, obviously." He took a step back, turning toward the water, a dark and endless expanse beyond the pale sand of the beach. "And I'm hoping, by tomorrow, whatever upset her at dinner will have cleared up. The guests will be arriving. She'll no doubt be distracted by that. And her dress."

Oh. Shit. "I'd forgotten all about that." I had a moment of panic, envisioning the dress still sitting on a runway in New York and Nathaniel shoving me out to sea in a rowboat. Or maybe he'd just make me swim. "But it will be here tomorrow, too."

"Unless the storm delays it." He looked away. Back at me. "I know James said it's not supposed to be a big storm, but you never know down here. Hopefully it'll just blow over; we'll have some rain, and that'll be the end of it. What time is the plane with the dress supposed to arrive?"

"Early afternoon, after lunch. If you're worried about it being delayed, aren't you worried about the guests too?"

This time, Ray's chuckle was flat. "For Emeline, I think the dress comes first. Her mother is set on the guest list of the century, but Emma is set on that dress. I want her to be happy. The dress will help."

Emma. It was the first time he'd called her that in front of me. Shannon, the bridesmaid, had called her Em, though, the nickname far more comfortable in her mouth than Emma was in Ray's. I wondered what that meant.

"I hope it does," I said.

"I should be going," Ray answered, the conversation ended just like that. We moved apart on the patio. I reached behind me and picked up his jacket, handed it to him.

"Thanks." He took it from me and stared down at it. For the space of a heartbeat, neither of us moved. Then, "I'll go back now. Thank you, Violet."

He moved down two steps and then turned, looking back at me. "Really," he added. "Thank you for listening. It's put a lot of things in perspective for me."

Before I could answer he was gone, walking into the darkness. The sky had clouded over, and the moon and stars were invisible overhead. I picked up the wine glasses and walked slowly back into my room, leaving the doors open. I wanted to listen to the ocean, fall asleep to the sound of the waves washing up on the beach. Maybe then I wouldn't feel so alone.

Most of my clothes were still tossed across the bed after my frantic search through my luggage for my suit. I dug around until I found my pajamas and the robe I'd worn earlier and then headed to the shower. My skin was sticky from the salt water and sand clung to my feet.

I stood under the warm water for a long time, letting it run through my hair, over my shoulders. I was tense, more than I thought I'd be. The buzz from the wine was long gone, burned off during the intensity of the kiss and by the guilt that was working its way through my mind and heart.

Maybe Ray was right—this was just a... moment. A mistake, a one-time thing. His life would go forward, and he'd marry Emeline. I'd do my job, try not to get fired. I wasn't that good at creating illusions, but I was going to have to build one big and heavy enough to cover what had happened. To make not only everyone else, but also myself, believe things were the same. That nothing had changed. Maybe that it hadn't happened at all.

I finally got out of the shower, wrapping one of the big fluffy towels around my hair and pulling on my pajamas. The wine was gone, the empty bottle on the tiny kitchen counter. I found some orange juice and poured a glass. It was tart and sweet and the best I'd ever tasted. Maybe people like Bartholomew could afford better orange juice than the rest of us. Or maybe everything just tasted better on a tropical island.

I sat cross-legged on the bed, sipping my juice. So much had happened in such a short time. I thought about tomorrow, how much there was to do, the dress. *Emeline's dress.*

And then, even though I didn't want to, I thought about Ray. And the kiss. I turned off the bedside light and slid down between the sheets, pulling the blanket up around my shoulders. Through the open door I could hear the waves falling against the sand, loud and no longer so tranquil. James had been right: there was a storm coming.

Chapter Eight

The next morning, the phone next to the bed rang while I was in the shower. I left a trail of soap across the bedroom floor as I lunged for it, wrapping a slick hand around the receiver and lifting it to my ear.

"Hello?"

"Violet. Darling. Where the hell are you?"

Nathaniel. "I was in the shower. What did you need?" I clutched the towel I'd grabbed on my way through the bathroom to my chest, trying to avoid standing in front of the open patio doors even though I doubted anyone would be strolling by so early in the morning. Especially after the bachelor party the guys had thrown for Ray.

"I want you to start tracking down that dress."

"We're an hour ahead of them," I reminded him. "No one's even there yet to call. As soon as they open, I promise I'll be on the phone."

There was a pause. "Fine," Nathaniel answered. "Then finish your shower. But I want you to make sure none of the guests arriving today have to wait. And it's raining, so you'll need to find an umbrella."

The line went dead. I sighed, and went back to the bathroom.

Twenty minutes later I was dressed and heading down the path toward the terminal. My cell phone, of course, had decided it didn't want to cooperate, so I wanted to ask Bartholomew if I could use the terminal phone to call the shipping company. I crossed my fingers that someone would be working in New York, able to take my call. And able to tell me what I wanted to hear, that the dress was going to be on the plane and the weather wasn't going to be a problem.

Currently the weather in question was a gentle rain, tropically warm. The breeze carried the scent of flowers and ocean, sweet and clean, all the stronger for the damp. It was so different from New York, where the rain hitting the hot sidewalk stirred up the smell of dirt and garbage, and truck fumes choked the air.

The pleasant woman behind the desk at the terminal dialed the number in New York for me and handed me the phone. Someone was there, and that someone had answers for me. The dress was packaged; the plane was chartered and was scheduled to leave on time. I asked about the storm, but they said it would be up to the pilot of the plane if things changed. I thanked them and hung up. I was almost to the terminal doors when I remembered and turned back.

"Do you know where I can find an umbrella?"

The receptionist did, and graciously handed me a huge umbrella the same color as the Hummer golf cart. I imagined there would be a Pearl Island logo to match when it unfurled.

My first guest of the day wasn't scheduled for another hour. I was trying to decide if I had time to find breakfast wherever the staff ate or if I should just head back to my room to ransack the little kitchen again, when the blare of static in my ear made me jump.

"Violet? Are you there?"

I tapped the mic. "I'm at the terminal. I just called..."

"I'm not asking about the dress. I need you at my villa, now."

He was gone. I sighed and caught the eye of the woman behind the desk. She gave me a sympathetic smile. I answered it with a somewhat rueful smile of my own and headed out into the rain.

It wasn't quite as far to Nathaniel's villa as it was to mine. A short while later, I was hopping out of the cart and jogging up the steps. He was out the door before I could even raise my arm to knock.

"I need a ride to the main villa," he said as he brushed past me.

I frowned. "Is something wrong with your cart?" I was only a few steps behind but he was already in mine, brushing a few stray raindrops from the fine weave of his suit jacket.

"Yes," he said without looking up, already deep in contemplation of contents pulled out of his ever-present leather-bound notebook.

I glanced at the cart and suppressed a laugh. The cord dangled from the front, plugged into nothing. I took a quick detour, reaching down to connect it to the outlet. As I stepped back from the cart, I heard a low hum.

"Sometime today, maybe?" Nathaniel called, leaning out of the cart. He quickly straightened back up as the soft rain hit his face, grimacing.

I scooted back around the end of the cart, taking my place behind the wheel.

"Just needed to be plugged in," I explained. "It should be charged pretty soon. I can bring you back later."

Nathaniel stared at me. "It wasn't plugged in?"

"Nope."

"Of all the silly things to forget." He shook his head. "You said you had an update on the dress?"

I nodded. "The shipping company confirmed the dress is there, packaged the way the bridal shop sent it, and it'll be on the plane as promised. Although there was a slight concern about the weather. The pilot has the final say as to whether or not it's safe to fly."

"Pray the weather holds out, then," Nathaniel answered. "When the dress arrives, find me and I'll take it to Emeline."

Once again I found myself nodding. We passed the rest of the brief ride in silence. I pulled up outside the main villa, then reached for the umbrella. Nathaniel, already out of the cart, waved it away.

I turned the cart around and headed back to the terminal. Apparently breakfast was out of the question, unless I could find something there.

As it turned out the woman behind the desk had a croissant and an orange juice, for which I was deeply grateful. I had just enough time to eat before the first flight of the day arrived.

The rest of the morning was spent meeting guests and taking them to their accommodations. I was honestly surprised by how many villas, rooms, and guest cottages were tucked away on the island. And I was amazed by the number of family members and friends attending the wedding, many of them just as prominent in the financial scene or the society pages as Raymond Rose and Emeline Brant.

Morning ticked on toward afternoon, the time for the charter to arrive from New York with Emeline's dress. Nothing had been delayed but the rain had continued steadily through the morning, the wind occasionally blowing gusts against the terminal windows.

With every arrival I tried to tell myself that, if they had made it through, the charter with the dress surely would. But as each of them turned out to be another plane full of guests, no dress in evidence, the reassurances felt more and more hollow.

"Stop worrying. No one's contacted us that the flight's not arriving."

Andi's reflection appeared beside me in the terminal glass where I stood, glued to the window, eyes on the sky.

"Do they do that? Do they let you know?"

Andi stood, looking up at the pewter-colored sky. "If they're on the schedule, yes, they'll let us know. And no one's contacted the terminal staff." She rested her hand on my shoulder. "So you can stop worrying."

"I'm not worried."

She met my gaze in the reflection. "Word of advice? Never—"

"Play poker," I finished, laughing. "I've heard that one before, actually."

"For good reason. Also, there." Andi pointed at the place where a darker gray spot had appeared against the clouds. It grew larger and larger, sinking lower over the tarmac, and then hit the runway, tires throwing up sprays of rainwater.

The plane rolled up in front of the terminal and stopped. Its stairs descended. I waited, tugging on the button of my blazer. Finally, after a long moment, a man appeared, a large, battered cardboard box under his arm. He struggled toward the terminal and I hurried to open the door.

"Thanks, Miss. Are you..." He juggled the box, trying to see the rain-spattered form on a clipboard he had wedged under his arm. I reached forward, sliding the board free, and held it up in front of him.

"No. I'm Violet Freesia. I called and arranged the flight. I'm with the wedding planner."

If he thought my name was strange, it didn't show on his face. He wrestled the box onto a nearby chair. "I need a signature confirming delivery."

I took the clipboard, signing the damp form where he pointed. When I handed it back he tore off a copy for me. I watched him run back through the rain to the waiting plane. The stairs retracted and the plane turned around, gaining speed as it went down the runway. Then it was airborne and gone.

Andi had already scooped up the box and was carrying it toward the door. "I'll put this in the cart," she said as I hurried after her.

"Thanks. And could I ask a favor?"

"Sure. What is it?"

"Nathaniel's cart is charging. Could someone drive it to the main villa for him? I think he'll need it."

"I'll see to it."

The rain was falling harder, and I ducked beneath the roof of the cart. Andi waved and ran back into the building.

I tried to raise Nathaniel on my mic, but there was just static. He'd wanted to deliver the dress to Emeline himself but I was much closer to

Emeline's villa than the main villa, where I'd left Nathaniel. I tried him again with still no result.

The sign for the Bliss Villa appeared and I turned down the path. The rain was falling steadily now and I parked as close as I could to the steps. There was no way I could handle the box and the umbrella both, so I bundled the box in my arms and carried it up to the porch.

I knocked, and there was a muffled noise from inside. The door didn't open. A minute passed, and I shifted the box in my arms as the weight grew more uncomfortable.

The door opened then. Mrs. Brant stood in the doorway, straight-backed as ever and dressed in a cream-colored suit. Emeline was behind her, dressed in a silky robe.

"Well, don't just stand there in the rain," she said shortly, sweeping the door open wider. "Come in."

"Finally." Emeline came forward as I stepped inside, hands grabbing the end of the box. I stumbled forward and we managed to set the box on the couch.

"Emeline," her mother said. "Please."

"Mother. It's my dress." Emeline's voice was tight.

"I can see that. But that doesn't mean you have to behave in such a ridiculous fashion."

"Please," Emeline said. "Mother."

We stood in that strange little tableau for a longer moment than I was comfortable with. Finally, I fumbled the packing slip out of my pocket and held it toward Emeline. Mrs. Brant stepped forward and snatched it from my hand. She scanned the paper with a narrow-eyed look.

"Emeline, you should open the box and inspect the dress for damage. The signature on this paper—" She rattled the packing slip in my direction, "means that you accept the dress as it is, and the box looks damaged. Let us hope the dress underneath is in pristine condition."

The look she directed at me with the words made it clear that she would hold me responsible if it wasn't.

Emeline, seemingly not even listening, was already prying the cover off the box and rifling through layer after layer of rose-colored tissue paper. She reached in, pulling out an armful of cream satin and beading, which she held up high, the long gown and train spilling out across the couch in a tumble of intricate gathers and beaded flowers.

"Oh. It's beautiful."

"Of course it is," Mrs. Brant snapped. "It should be, given what it cost. But it's completely impractical for a beach wedding."

"It's the dress I wanted," Emeline said, sounding on the edge of tears.

"I'm not having this discussion with you right now," her mother answered coldly. "I can see where it's headed. It's here. You have your wish. Now you get to live with it."

Emeline's eyes filled with the tears I'd heard in her voice, and my heart went out to her. What would it be like to have a mother who was so cold? My own mother and I had always been close. She'd have shared every minute of my wedding plans with me and been happy just because I was.

"Well?" her mother said. "Are you going to try it on?"

"Of course I am," Emeline said. The tears had dried up. She scooped the dress back into her arms and headed to her bedroom with a rustle of silk.

I glanced toward the door, not sure if I should leave. Mrs. Brant caught my eye, and I decided it was better to stay. Most likely she wanted me around to yell at if for some reason the dress wasn't completely perfect.

She didn't speak. I didn't quite dare to. I could hear the rain tapping against the windows. The minutes passed in silence, feeling longer than they were. I glanced up at the ceiling, looking for the expanse of glass Ray's villa had, but this room had only a steeply-pitched wooden ceiling with a large fan. I was still looking up when the bedroom door opened.

Emeline stood in the muted watery light from the window. She was absolutely stunning, even with her hair pulled back and no makeup on. The dress was strapless, beautifully draped and pleated. A wash of beaded flowers ran across the front below the nipped-in waist, down the side, and in a sweep across the train.

"I need your help," she said to her mother.

When she turned, the back of her dress was a complicated tangle of satin ties. Her mother, expression empty of anything charitable, got up and began to tighten the ties from the top, yanking them sharply enough that Emeline pulled in a sharp intake of breath.

"This should go tighter," her mother said after a moment. "It's too big."

"I've probably lost weight."

"Hmm." Her mother didn't sound convinced. She stepped back, eying the dress, and Emeline, critically.

Emeline swept past her in a wave of satin, striding to the full-length mirror in the corner of the room, and stood staring into it, the tilt of her mouth strangely sad.

"There's a spot on the back of the dress." Her mother had followed her across the room.

Emeline and I both looked down at the cream satin.

"Where?" Emeline asked.

"There." Her mother pointed with one manicured nail. "On the edge of the train."

I moved in closer, kneeling to see what she was pointing at as Emeline twisted around to look, too. There was, in fact, a spot, slightly darker than the area around it.

"I think it's just water," I offered.

"Just water," Mrs. Brant echoed, voice like ice.

She stalked across the room to the box the dress came in and pawed through the tissue, tossing it onto the floor until she found what she was looking for. She held up one crumpled sheet. The rose-colored tissue in the bottom right was colored deep magenta with water. Mrs. Brant flipped the box over. The back was crumpled, one corner damaged. Clearly wet.

"This is how the dress got wet." She stabbed a finger at the offending box. "It's ruined, and it's your fault."

I glanced over at Emeline, who looked back at me without expression.

"The box was—"

"I'm not interested in your excuses," Mrs. Brant snapped.

"Violet," Emeline said, her voice soft against the sharp edges of her mother's, "call Nathaniel."

"That would be an excellent idea," her mother said. "By all means, get Nathaniel on the phone."

I tapped my ear piece. "Nathaniel? Are you there?"

The familiar burst of static greeted me. "I'm here. I'm busy. What is it?"

"There's a problem with Emeline's dress."

"Don't tell me it hasn't arrived."

"No. It's here. It's just—"

"Just tell him I want him here. Now." Emeline met my eyes, and I thought I read apology in her eyes. "Can you just tell him that?"

"Emeline would like you to come to the villa," I relayed to Nathaniel.

"Then you'll have to come get me. I have no working cart, remember?"

"Andi brought one for you. It should be parked outside." There was silence. I waited but there was nothing more.

"Well?" Mrs. Brant asked.

"He's on his way."

"This is unacceptable. The dress is ruined and it doesn't fit her."

"The spot is barely noticeable," I said, trying to soothe the agitation in the room. "Let it dry out, and the guests will never know it was even there."

"And what," Mrs. Brant demanded, "would you know about it? You're just the wedding planner's assistant."

I know that what should matter in a wedding is love. Not all of these trappings. I wasn't stupid enough to say that to Vivienne Brant's face. I held up my hands, palm out. "I'm just here to help, Mrs. Brant."

"Yes. Well. You're failing quite spectacularly at that."

I choked on the words that wanted to rise in answer to that, and was saved by a brisk knock at the door. Nathaniel. I'd never been so glad to see him. He pushed past me into the villa, took one look at the room and shoved me outside, the door closing firmly at my back. I wasn't even mad that he hadn't bothered to speak to me. All I wanted to be was away from that woman.

Clattering down the steps, I hopped into my cart and gladly left.

Chapter Nine

Driving back toward the terminal, I tried to shake off the weight of gloom that had settled on my shoulders. It was obvious Vivien Brant was not the kind of woman who ever saw anyone else as worthy of her time. I shouldn't have let her get to me. But brushing off her comments was easier thought than done.

It wasn't, I reminded myself, as though I was completely incompetent at my job—the less than professional interactions with Ray aside. I had a general idea of what I was doing. And a single water spot along the hem of the wedding dress, where no one would ever see it, was not the end of the damn world. Vivien hadn't even liked the dress! Though I got the feeling that, whatever she thought of Emeline's choices regarding the wedding, she wanted the illusion of perfection even in the things she disapproved of. Wanted a wedding that the society rags would gush over for weeks to come.

The path curved sharply and I slowed, driving carefully on the damp pavement. Someone called my name. I skidded to a stop on the corner, cart swerving on the water that covered the road and heart racing. Almost running someone over would be just what my reputation needed.

"Sorry," the voice said, and I recognized it even before Ray came up from behind the cart. My heart skipped for an entirely different reason than fear. "I keep sneaking up on you. Are you okay?"

He sounded a little breathless, and he was dressed in running shorts and shoes. And nothing else. His hair was damp from the rain, his face flushed. He stood on the path beside the cart, hands on his hips, catching his breath. He watched me expectantly for a long moment before I realized that I was staring at him and not answering his question.

"Oh. Yeah. I'm fine." I took a breath and tried to calm the too-fast beating of my heart. "You caught me by surprise, is all. The only person I've seen walk anywhere around here was your grandfather yesterday."

Ray laughed. "Grandpa Drew would walk around the world if he could." He shook his damp hair back from his face and leaned in closer, hands braced against the roof of the cart. I tried to remember how breathing worked. "He used to take me on these long walks. Rambles, he called them. When I was a kid we'd visit England, and there are these walking trails in the Cotswolds. You can go for miles over the hills, walk all day, and then stay in an inn at one of the little villages. We'd wake up the next morning, eat these huge breakfasts at the inn, get a packed lunch, and then start walking again. It was beautiful."

His face was alive with the memory, his eyes dancing. The excitement was contagious, and I smiled. "It sounds like it. How old were you?"

He tapped his fingertips against the roof in thought for a moment. "We started the walk when I was about seven, I think. Just day walks. I went every summer, though, and by the time I was in my teens we'd be out for a week or longer."

"Do you still go back?"

"Not since the summer before college," Ray answered, shaking his head. "Life got in the way, I guess."

"Maybe you can take Emeline there now. Start a new tradition."

"Emeline isn't much for hiking," Ray said, shrugging. "But I'm sure she wouldn't object to a trip to England. Maybe a night or two in one of the inns where Grandpa and I used to stay."

There was one of those semi-awkward pauses, the silence stretching out between us. Ray was still leaning on the roof of the cart, looking down at me. I looked up at him, and wanted words. Something profound. Or at least something that could keep the conversation going.

The little thrill that always went through me when I saw him was still thrumming in my bones, and as much as I knew he belonged to someone else it was too soon to let go of that feeling.

"Emeline's dress arrived," I said, grasping at straws for something to say. "I just dropped it off."

"I imagine that made her happy."

I winced, and quickly rearranged my face. It was too late, though. He had already seen. His smile dimmed.

"What happened?"

A sigh escaped before I could catch it back. "The dress had a water spot; the box must have been damaged, and the rain got the tissue paper wet. Emeline was reasonable enough about it, but her mother..."

Ray shook his head. "Mrs. Brant is a very intense woman. Don't let her get to you."

"The problem is, if she says the wrong thing to Nathaniel I could lose my job."

His expression tightened. "I'd be more than happy to remind Nathaniel that my future mother-in-law is not the one who hired him. I am."

That wasn't exactly the response I'd expected. Or one I wanted to inspire. "I don't think that's necessary," I said quickly. "I'm sure it's just... Well. The dress is the one thing Emeline seems set on, and all mothers want their daughters to be happy on their wedding day, right? Besides, this wedding's big enough. Lots of guests. And stress can make people a little sharp."

Ray looked at me for long enough that I feared he could see just how just how fake the words tasted on my tongue. He lay a hand on my shoulder. "You're sweet, Violet. And..." He sighed. "I wish you were right. I guess the good news is that it's Emeline I'm marrying and not her mother."

"I guess I just want everyone to be happy." I gave him a smile that I hoped looked encouraging.

I couldn't say what I wanted to, that it didn't seem like either he or Emeline were looking forward to the wedding—or the marriage—the way a bride and groom should. And that once he married her daughter, Vivien Brant would never stop using their relationship as leverage. Even knowing what I knew, everything James and Ione had hinted at, everything Ray had told me himself, I had a responsibility. I was meant to be the wedding planner's assistant. There needed to be a wedding actually happening for that to stay true. And... It wasn't my place. Wanting him didn't make Ray mine. He was a grown man, and more than likely well aware of what he was getting himself into.

"I should be letting you work," Ray said, his smile a little sad.

"And I should let you get out of the rain," I answered, though I wanted nothing more than to take him with me.

"At least it's a warm rain. In New York I'd be miserable. This..." He held out his hands and lifted his face to the sky. "This is wonderful."

"As long as you're happy," I said, giving him a look more dubious than I actually felt, hoping to coax out a real smile. "Despite the fact that I think you're a little crazy."

The teasing tone won me a laugh, and the sound of it warmed the place in my chest that felt hollow with the anticipation of his absence.

"I am," he said. And then again, more to himself than to me, "I am." He looked up, as though remembering that I was still there. He smiled at me and then he jogged a few steps backward, eyes fixed on my face, before he turned and headed for his villa.

I watched him for a moment, arms relaxed, broad shoulders, long legs taking him down the path away from me. The warm feeling I'd felt while we'd talked slowly left me, replaced with a sense of loss that didn't entirely make sense.

How could I lose someone who didn't belong to me?

Chapter Ten

I tried to avoid Ray's side of the island, as I'd come to think of it, after that. My feelings were tangled and raw, and I wasn't sure I could manage seeing him again without spilling them out everywhere. He didn't deserve that, and I couldn't afford to risk my job any more than I already had.

Thankfully, most of the guests were in rooms and cottages close to the terminal, so I hadn't needed to venture too far. But the more guests who arrived, the further I'd traveled across the island—and the closer I came to Ray's villa. I wasn't sure if he was even there, or what the plans were for him and his groomsmen for the afternoon. It hadn't occurred to me to ask him. They were likely on one of the documents in the folder Nathaniel had given me, but I knew if I looked it would only make the temptation to go find him stronger. It wasn't my job to know where the groom's party was. I needed to focus on what *was* my responsibility.

It was well past lunch when the last chartered flight of guests arrived. Most of them, despite their positions in the social register and the number of zeroes that must have been in their bank accounts, were nice enough. Apparently only the bride's mother felt the need to maintain her status by stepping on everyone else. That, or I hadn't pissed off any of them yet. I ferried them to their villas and then checked in with Nathaniel, who informed me that I was done for the day but to keep my mic on just in case.

The rehearsal dinner was that night, for the guests as well as the bridal party. Again, it would be handled by the island staff, with Nathaniel overseeing, who apparently didn't need an assistant for such things. And that was okay with me. I had the distinct sense Nathaniel would somehow press me into waiting tables, and I'd done enough of that during college.

As I headed back toward my little slice of the island the paths were slick with rain, puddles of water collecting in the dips and hollows. I'd splashed myself more than once, and one leg of my pants was wet up to the knee. All I wanted right now was a hot shower and dry clothes.

I turned down the path to my villa, looking forward to some wine and another dinner of bread and cheese. I laughed. Bread and cheese, back home with Lydia, would have been the desperation meal the day before payday. But here the cheese had names I couldn't pronounce, and the bread was thick and dense and full of flavor. It might have been a simple repast, but it sure wasn't poor.

The rain had let up, the sky lightening. I hoped it meant the storm was passing over. I pulled up to the cart plug and stepped out onto the wet grass. I was just plugging the cart in when static erupted in my ear. I dropped the plug and jumped back from it, half expecting a jolt of electricity to shoot up my arm.

Then the burst of static solidified into Nathaniel's voice. "Violet. Where are you?"

I sighed, and pulled on a professional voice. Apparently I was not about to get another evening to myself. "I'm at my villa. What's up?" I plugged in the cart and ran up the steps to the door. Even though the rain had stopped, the wind had picked up and it was getting cooler.

"I need you at the main villa. There's a problem with the seating arrangements for the dinner. I'm working with the kitchen and wait staff right now, so you'll have to handle it."

"I need a few minutes to change. My clothes are wet."

"Wear a dress if you're changing. Something nice, yes? Just in case you're here during the actual dinner."

I glanced at my suitcase. The nicest dress I'd brought was borrowed from Lydia and I hadn't bothered to unpack it, figuring I'd be wearing business casual right up to the end.

"Sure. I'll be there as soon as I can, Nathaniel."

He was gone. I grabbed the dress, a silky green thing Lydia had insisted went well with my complexion. She'd also sent along a pair of decent strappy heels, black, not too terribly high, but I still liked them quite a bit. It wasn't often I got to dress up in anything more daring than close-toed pumps.

But the dress was wrinkled. More than I knew Nathaniel would tolerate. I glanced at my watch. I'd give Nathaniel twenty minutes before he started looking for me.

Taking the dress in hand, I made a dash for the bathroom, turning on the shower. I hung the dress on the back of the door and closed the door. I did a quick dance beneath the warm water, got out of the shower, and turned the hot water on full force. I slipped out with a pile of towels and the hairdryer, closing the door behind me. Hopefully the hot water would generate enough steam to ease some of the wrinkles out of the dress.

I sat on the bed, wrapped in towels, and dried my hair. There wasn't much I could do with it, other than straighten it as much as possible with my brush, but that wasn't working. The humidity had done a number on it, and it had become an out-of-control mass floating around my head. I had an inspired idea and managed to wrangle it into a semi-controlled chignon at the back of my neck. Some stray tendrils escaped and I let them air- dry. As I'd expected, they curled into little ringlets.

Typically, I wore a brush of mascara and a fairly sedate lipstick, but Lydia had insisted I take along most of her collection of eye shadow. I added it to the usual basics after some consideration.

Digging through my luggage I found clean lingerie and slipped into it, heading back to the bathroom. When I opened the door, I was enveloped in a cloud of steam. Leaving the door open, I turned off the hot water and rescued the dress. In the steam-free air of the bedroom, I held it up. The wrinkles were gone, the dress nice and smooth. I had no illusions it would stay that way, but at least I was starting the evening wrinkle-free.

The dress was definitely Lydia's style. And size. I wasn't curvy by anyone's standards, but the clinging fabric definitely did show off what was there. I smoothed the dress over my hips in front of the full-length mirror on the back of the bathroom door and regarded my reflection with a critical gaze.

I hadn't done too badly. The face looking back at me wasn't quite what I usually saw there, but I couldn't say I didn't look pretty. There was a bit more of me exposed than I was used to, though. The deep neckline of the dress put things on display I hadn't shown off since I kicked Evan out.

There was a hibiscus growing outside my door. I stepped out and picked a flower, marveling at the color, hot pink at the center that shaded to orange at the edges. I tucked the bloom into my hair behind my ear, took one last look in the mirror, and pronounced myself as good as it would get.

I unplugged the cart and slid carefully onto the seat, trying hard not to wrinkle the dress, then drove at a sedate pace to the main villa, avoiding puddles as carefully as though they contained acid. There was no way I was getting this dress, or the shoes, wet.

When I arrived Nathaniel was on the steps of the villa, and his eyebrows went sharply upward as he took in my appearance. Then, surprising me, he smiled. "Not what I would have expected from you, Violet."

I guess I should have been less shocked to get that compliment from a man in harem pants and a linen tunic.

We headed inside, and Nathaniel handed me a seating chart. "Mrs. Brant was here early," he said as he gave it over, sounding more than a little put out. "She demanded everything be changed."

The chart I had in my folder of plans showed neatly-labeled tables. This one looked like the playbook for a football team—with arrows, marks, and crosses peppering the page.

"Each guest has a name tag," Nathaniel added, "and they need to be moved."

As we entered the main dining room, I glanced up and stopped. The room was enormous, with dozens of small round tables scattered across the polished teak floor. Each table held small crystal bowls with flowers floating in them and groupings of small candles in crystal holders. The candles weren't lit yet; the dinner was still a few hours away. Everyone was still at the rehearsal, in the building where the ceremony would be held, or lounging around their villas. I glanced at Nathaniel and had the sinking feeling after I'd untangled the seating chart, I'd be set to lighting candles.

"I need to go back to the rehearsal and check on Emeline. See how things are going." Nathaniel was consulting a piece of paper, which he then shoved at me. "I'm trusting you to follow up with the kitchen staff as well. See that they're ready to start serving promptly at a quarter past seven."

I nodded, glancing down at the menu. It all sounded wonderful, lots of fresh fish and other types of seafood—no doubt locally caught—vegetables, and then desserts. All the desserts. Someone had a sweet tooth. I smiled, imagining it was probably Ray. Somehow I couldn't imagine Emeline indulging in all that refined sugar.

Nathaniel was gone by the time I looked up again, the sound of his footsteps fading as he headed down the hall. I set the menu aside and looked at the seating arrangement, trying to decide where to start. It was a little overwhelming.

"You look like you're thinking pretty hard about something."

I spun around toward the voice behind me. Ray was there, leaning against the doorframe. He looked relaxed and at ease, hands in his pockets, smiling at me.

"I thought you were at the rehearsal. How long have you been standing there?"

He straightened, walking toward me. "Long enough to see you need some help."

"Is it that obvious?"

Ray just grinned, and I looked down at the seating chart and the nearly-incomprehensible edits that someone—presumably Mrs. Brant—had added to the formerly organized setup. "Yeah. Okay. I guess it is."

"Here." He was standing next to me, then, close enough that I could feel the warmth of his arm next to mine. "Let me see."

I tried to concentrate on what he was saying. He was speaking again, no doubt offering some kind of plan, but I lost him after the first few words. Almost without me deciding to do it, my body leaned in toward his until the fabric of his shirt touched my bare skin.

The thrill that ran through me was immediate and intense. And it scared me. I was tempting fate, playing with fire, all those euphemisms that meant I should be paying attention to my job and not someone else's fiancé. There was nothing good that could come of this. We'd had a kiss, but that was it. It had been a mistake and it wasn't likely to be repeated.

"Okay, Violet? Does that make sense?" I looked up at Ray and found his blue eyes on mine.

"I'm sorry. I was..." How could I tell him I was distracted by his cologne? Or his warmth? Or... him?

"Here. Let's make this simple. Pick up all these." He started picking up the little name tags from the nearest table. "And we'll just start from scratch, okay?"

I nodded and we moved around the room, picking up the little engraved cards. There seemed to be no end to them. Ray stopped to grab a wicker bread basket from the buffet table.

"Here." He held it toward me and I dumped my cards into it, adding them to his.

"There," he said when we were done. "It should be easy enough sorting things out now."

Frankly, I didn't understand why Mrs. Brant had felt the need to re-arrange the entire seating chart in the first place. Clearly she had some kind of issue with Ray's grandmother, but it would have been a simple enough fix to just change her own seat. Or, if she was going to be nasty about it, Ione's. She didn't need to re-seat the entire dining room.

We went to the first table on the list, sorting through the tags in the basket until we found the ones we were looking for. I arranged them by each place setting, careful to put them down exactly as they'd been before we picked them up, directly above each dinner plate. Nathaniel would notice if they weren't, and no doubt Mrs. Brant had chosen the placement specifically or something and would throw a fit if they weren't properly aligned.

When that first table was done, we moved on to the next. Ray told me stories about the names on the cards as we worked, about how this uncle had once had dinner with some titled nobleman, or the cousin who liked to rebuild old cars. There seemed to be far more cards for his family and friends than for Emeline's, and I asked him about it as we worked our way through the room.

He sighed. "Emeline is an only child. Mrs. Brant never remarried after her father died, and she didn't have any siblings either. Which means no aunts or uncles, or cousins. There's family on her father's side, but I guess they had a falling out and Emeline never really met any of them. As for friends, beyond her bridal party I don't think Emeline really has many. She's shy, and she doesn't connect very easily with other people."

Ray was looking down at one of the name cards. He'd been tracing the engraving over and over with his fingers as he talked, like he wasn't entirely comfortable with the subject. "Emeline hasn't had an easy life;

I think I mentioned that to you. Her mother moved her from boarding school to boarding school when she was younger. I think she went to at least four."

"But why did she move her so often?" Even if they had moved frequently, she was already going away for school. It seemed strange that her mother wouldn't just keep her at whichever school she'd started in.

"Nothing ever really satisfied Vivien." It was the first time I'd heard Ray call his future mother-in-law by her given name. He spoke like he still wasn't quite sure about the way it felt in his mouth. "She was always looking for a better school. Better teachers. She used to get in arguments with the staff over the most ridiculous things. Emeline won't tell you how much her mother put on her shoulders, but Shannon said once that she used to take Adderall to get through all her classes and extracurriculars."

He finally looked up and met my eyes. "This whole thing... the wedding, all the high-society posturing, it's just one more thing Emeline is doing to please her mother. My hope is that once it's done she'll finally be satisfied for a while. That maybe she'll finally give Emeline some space to breathe."

I thought of his grandmother telling me that Ray was trying to save Emeline, and couldn't help but agree with Ione in that moment. Whatever he really wanted, he was going to put it aside because he thought he had to rescue Emeline from her mother. And I had to let him, because I was just the wedding planner's assistant.

"How did you two meet?" *How did all of this start?* I'd heard the short version from his grandmother, but I wanted to hear his side of it. Wanted to know if there had been any point in the relationship where they both truly wanted a wedding. We started moving between tables again, setting out more cards.

"Emeline was volunteering for a charity," Ray said. "One I donated a great deal of money to. Helping women in impoverished areas set up businesses of their own. That sort of thing. Honestly, I think Emeline started working there because Shannon was. But she does genuinely care."

He set out another card. "Anyway, she'd organized a dinner dance, very formal, for donors. I wasn't dating anyone at the time and Emeline, well, I think she had feelings for someone else. Or she'd had feelings. But she won't talk about it, even now. We spent most of the evening together, and when I called her the next day she agreed to go out with me."

The words hung, waiting, but Ray didn't speak. I didn't feel like there was a place for me to. It felt like interrupting.

Finally, Ray said, "I fell in love with her."

Or he thought he had. He'd said as much before.

"And she with you?" I asked. I held his gaze, and he dropped his gaze. Silence fell between us once more, full of unspoken words.

"Violet!"

I jumped, the basket jerking in my hands, and some of the name cards spilled out onto the floor. Nathaniel was standing in the doorway of the villa, Emeline just coming up the steps behind him.

"Nathaniel." I could hear the breathless shock in my own voice. Knew that I must look as though I'd been caught doing something wrong. "We were just..."

Just what? Just talking? The words somehow felt more like a confession than a denial of wrongdoing.

"I asked you to set up the tables. Not bother Ray."

"It's fine, Nathaniel. I volunteered to help her." He glanced past Nathaniel to Emeline, and if he'd intended to say anything else he swallowed the words.

"Violet is quite capable of taking care of it herself, I'm sure," Nathaniel said.

I wanted to reach out for Ray. To lay a hand on his arm. But I knew what a stupid thing that would be to do in front of the woman he was about to marry. I reached for the little card in his hand instead. "I think I can take this from here."

Our fingers brushed briefly, a little tingle running through me, and I smiled. And then I caught Emeline's gaze, her green eyes watching me from where she stood in the shadow of the doorway. Despite knowing what I knew, I half expected a narrow-eyed glare. The kind of look a woman, even one who wasn't in love with the man she was about to marry, might give the person she caught flirting with her groom-to-be. Instead she just looked... sad.

"Thanks for your help, Ray." I dropped the card into the basket and backed away as gracefully as I could. Not sure what to make of everything that had just happened, and not wanting to hold any more attention that I'd already attracted.

I started placing name cards at the next table. Nathaniel had gone back to the kitchen, presumably to check on the progress with dinner. When I glanced up from the place setting I'd just finished, Emeline was standing with her hand in Ray's, her palm against his cheek. I hadn't heard her speak, but there was something passing between them. They looked... intimate. My chest ached and I turned away, moving on to the next table.

Chapter Eleven

Outside, the sound of wind and rain had grown louder, and I hoped the storm wasn't getting stronger. It occurred to me that if the weather deteriorated any further, I might spend the rest of my night ferrying guests back and forth between the main villa and their personal accommodations. I moved on to the next table, digging through the basket for another card.

The sound of people attempting to argue in whispers pulled my attention up. Emeline and Ray were halfway across the room, but it was easy to see that they were the culprits. Emeline's expression was tight, her face turned up to Ray and her lips pressed thin. She was clearly upset, but I wasn't entirely sure who with. Maybe the look she'd given me earlier had just been a marker of restraint. The kind of people who ended up in the society pages probably had to learn early on to keep a straight face under pressure.

Ray shook his head, as tense as Emeline was. He ran a hand through his hair and dropped it back to his side.

"I don't know what to tell you." His words just barely reached me. "What did you want me to do?"

"I don't know," Emeline snapped back. "I just—" She dropped her face into her hands, her shoulders rising and falling with a shuddering breath. When she raised her head, she looked defeated. "She's going to have her way about it. And that's that."

"Emma," Ray said, the first time I'd ever heard him use a pet name for her. "Why..."

He seemed to give up on whatever he'd been about to say, raising a hand again to rub at the back of his neck.

"You know why," Emeline said, and whether she was answering the unfinished why or the unspoken question behind it, that seemed to be the end of the conversation. She turned and walked away.

For a moment Ray stood there looking after her, and then he turned toward me. I quickly looked away, fumbling with the cards, but I wasn't quite fast enough. He caught my eye and crossed the room.

"Everything okay?" I asked as he pulled out a chair and dropped down into it, shoulders slumped.

"She's tired," Ray said. "And a bit stressed. We both are. And her mother has been... Emeline was caught up for so long at rehearsal because she insisted on going through every little aspect of the schedule with her. I think they had some kind of argument. Not even sure what about. But it's put Emma on edge."

And there it was again. Emma. I supposed it wasn't that strange. They were about to be married, after all. But the tenderness was unexpected after how staid their relationship had seemed.

"Weddings take a lot of out of people," I said, but even I could tell that the words rang hollow.

Ray's smile looked as fake as mine felt. "Tell me about it." He dropped the smile an instant later and sighed. "It's more than that, though. Usually with weddings you have, well, the sort of fairytale romance thing. I'm sure you've guessed ours isn't that."

"I—" What could I say to him? Of course I had. But I couldn't give that answer, and I was sure he knew it. Even if I were willing to, with my luck Nathaniel would walk in on me encouraging a client to leave his bride at the altar and fire me on the spot. I took a deep breath.

"Whatever you have to say, Violet, please say it. You're not going to make me angry. Chances are I've already heard it."

I shook my head, setting out a couple more cards as I walked around the table toward Ray. "It's not really my place."

He rose from the chair, stopping my progress around the table. His eyes, when they caught and held mine, were suspiciously bright. "Violet. Please."

For once, Nathaniel's interruption came at a completely opportune moment.

"Violet!" The call came from down the hall, toward the kitchen. "Are you finished with those seat assignments?"

I spun around, thankfully not dropping the basket of cards I held. "Just wrapping up the last table."

"You'll need to light the candles next," Nathaniel said, appearing in the doorway. "There's not much time before guests will start arriving. And you still need to go collect the grandparents." He paused, realizing Ray was standing here. "Oh. Ray. Did you need something?"

"Actually, I was just asking Violet a bit of a favor."

I was sure all the color had drained from my face. He wasn't going to tell Nathaniel what he'd just asked me. He couldn't. I held my breath, sure Nathaniel wouldn't react well to me slapping my hand over Ray's mouth.

"I wanted to borrow her cart. I think I'd like to get my grandparents myself, if you don't mind."

"It's really no trouble for Violet to get them," Nathaniel said, darting a look between us.

"I'd really rather do it. Grandpa will just try to walk if Violet shows up, rain and all." He smiled charmingly. "I think I can get him to submit to the cart."

Nathaniel shrugged. "It's your wedding. Do what you like. The cart is charged, Violet?"

"Completely."

Ray brushed his fingertips against my arm and I looked down, trying to keep my expression neutral as the touch sent a shock of electricity through me. "I'll bring it back in one piece."

We watched him leave, and Nathaniel turned to me. For the first time, his expression was something like gentle.

"Nothing good is going to come out of that," he said, his tone making it very clear that he wasn't going to accept any dissembling.

I ran a hand over my face, remembering too late that I was wearing makeup and hoping I hadn't smudged it. "I know," I said. "I swear I'm not encouraging it, Nathaniel. I don't know what—"

He held up a hand, cutting me off. "I know you think I'm harsh," he said. "And I probably have been. We met in the middle of the biggest wedding I've ever coordinated. I'm only human. Stress gets to me just like anybody else."

I stared at him. It wasn't that I thought Nathaniel was incapable of being reasonable. I'd seen him be more than on several occasions; he'd handled Mrs. Brant's outbursts better than anyone else. But I hadn't expected this conversation.

"What I'm saying is that all of us are still just people, and sometimes we have feelings we don't have complete control over. We just do the best we can and we carry on."

"Yeah," I agreed, still a little stunned. "Of course."

"Good. So, while you're carrying on, light the candles. Emeline and I are going to get her mother."

He spun on his heel and swanned off into the kitchen. I stared after him for a shocked heartbeat before I shook myself out of my funk and turned back to the tables. The wait staff was starting to set up the dinner buffet, using butane lighters to light the little burners beneath the chafing dishes. They were more than happy to let me borrow one, and I made quick work of the candles without the admittedly very pleasant distraction of Ray at my side.

When the candles were lit, the soft glow of them caught the facets in the glasses and made the china plates gleam. It looked romantic and cozy, even in the large room, and I thought that even Mrs. Brant couldn't be displeased with that.

The doors opened, and Ray ushered his grandmother in. The two of them were arm in arm and she was laughing up at him, looking quite delighted with whatever he'd just said. She caught my eye as her laughter faded and was quickly across the room, pressing a kiss to each of my cheeks.

"Violet. How lovely to see you, dear."

"And you," I said, smiling genuinely back at her. Ione, at least, was easy. "Where's Drew?" I wondered if he'd decided to walk after all.

"Parking the cart," Ione said, with a sigh that would have been long-suffering if she hadn't sounded so amused. "He insisted on driving. It's a miracle we made it here in one piece."

I laughed. "He discovered the top speed, I assume?"

Ray was still laughing. "If you think I was bad, you should ride along with Grandpa sometime. I think he took the corners on two wheels."

"Your grandfather does enjoy a bit of speed," Ione chuckled. "Has he ever told you about the time he and Bartholomew—"

A crash behind us cut off the story before it could begin. Nathaniel came through the doors, ushering Emeline and Mrs. Brant in before him. All three were disheveled and wet, Emeline's thin silk dress clinging to every curve and her hair hanging in damp tendrils around her face. Nathaniel's linen tunic dripped water onto the floor. Mrs. Brant looked livid. Both of them had raccoon rings of smudged makeup around their eyes.

"Emma. What happened?" Ray crossed the space between himself and Emeline in three long strides and then hesitated, like he wasn't sure whether or not to touch her.

"The cart is what happened." Despite resembling nothing quite so much as a drowned rat Emeline's mother stood ramrod straight, her steely gaze sweeping the room. The buffet staff seemed to have vanished, all of them neatly out of reach of her wrath. Her eyes landed on me and narrowed. "I suspect it was your responsibility to see that the cart was in working order."

It wasn't a question.

I looked wide-eyed at Nathaniel. It was his cart.

"I thought the whole experience was refreshing," he said, breezy as anything.

"Refreshing!" Mrs. Brant advanced on him, and he looked like he was abruptly regretting the blasé attitude that, up to that point, had more or less gotten him through the rough spots.

I wasn't sure what would have happened if the door hadn't opened just at that moment, admitting a group of laughing men and women. They seemed oblivious to the rain, despite all looking a little damp around the edges. If I'd had to guess, I would have said the flushed cheeks and jovial attitudes had been helped along by a few drinks. It seemed like James' style.

Several of the bridesmaids gasped at the sight of Emeline. Shannon stepped out from the huddle of them, wearing a short dress of sea-foam green chiffon, her dark braids coiled into an elegant knot. Emeline all but collapsed into her arms, hiding her face against her maid-of-honor's shoulder. Shannon seemed completely un-bothered by the water soaking into her own dress from Emeline's. Her hand stroked over Emeline's soaked hair, and she was murmuring something I couldn't catch into the other girl's ear.

"You," Mrs. Brant said, her ire apparently directed at me once more. "I want to talk to you."

"I'll speak with her," Nathaniel said. "Don't trouble yourself with an assistant, Vivien. Give me just a moment and we'll head back to the villa so you and Emeline can change."

Before Mrs. Brant or I could protest, Nathaniel had caught me by the arm and ushered me off to the side.

"What happened?" I asked as soon as we were out of earshot of the wedding party.

"The cart died on the path. In the rain." Nathaniel sounded a little like he was trying not to laugh. "Honestly, I thought Vivien was going to become the first provable case of spontaneous combustion." His expression lost the amusement. "But unfortunately she needs someone to blame, and she seems to have decided that's you."

"It was your cart," I reminded him, emboldened by how understanding he'd been earlier.

"I'm not the one eye-fucking her daughter's fiancé," Nathaniel retorted, not unkindly.

That was... fair. If a bit blunt. Past Nathaniel's shoulder I could see more guests arriving, several of them carrying umbrellas. The groomsmen had gone off out of eyesight, most of the bridesmaids with them, but Emeline and Shannon were still standing where we'd left them—Mrs. Brant, Ray, and his grandparents gathered close around. Ray, I thought, looked a little at a loss.

"I see your point," I said.

"I have to go deal with this. You start seating the guests. And try to be unobtrusive about it."

"Okay. I'll take care of things here." I turned to go but he caught my arm again, just tightly enough to get my attention.

"Vivien is watching you, Violet. Which means you can't be hanging around Ray. He needs to be giving his attention to Emeline."

If anything, *Ray* had been hanging around *me*. I almost said as much, but the look on Nathaniel's face stopped me. It wasn't a threat, I reminded myself. What Nathaniel was telling me was a warning, and he was right.

"If she catches you mooning after him like a lovesick calf, I won't be able to save your job."

"I understand," I made myself say.

He nodded sharply. "Good." And then he was gone. I watched him lead Emeline out, Shannon going with them, her arm still around the bride's shoulders.

Mrs. Brant didn't follow. It seemed she was going to push through the rest of the evening in her damp clothes. I didn't particularly look forward to dealing with that.

Being unobtrusive likely didn't include approaching or speaking to the woman who'd decided to make me the scapegoat for everything that went wrong with her daughter's wedding. I crossed the room to Ray and his grandparents instead, though not too soon to miss overhearing Emeline's mother order a double shot of whiskey, neat. Apparently, she was a little human after all.

Chapter Twelve

"Ione," I said, approaching her. "Drew. Would you like to be seated?"

"Yes, dear," Ione said. "Thank you."

She hooked her arm through mine and I smiled, steering her and, by extension, her husband, toward their seats. Drew pulled Ione's chair out and she daintily sat down in it, smiling up at him. A server approached and began to explain the dinner selections, asking them what they'd like to drink.

"—not exactly being subtle," I heard a half-familiar voice say, pitched low so it wouldn't carry.

I half turned, and saw James and two of the other groomsmen standing close together off to one side. James shook his head, and I sidled a little closer under the pretense of checking one of the table arrangements.

"The people who know, know. The rest won't see. Or won't want to."

I waited a moment, but there was nothing else. They'd apparently decided the conversation was too risky. I wondered what they could have been referring to as I moved toward the door. Ray and Emeline, surely. It was, after all, a little blatant that Emeline had gone to her maid of honor rather than her husband-to-be for comfort. But I didn't have time to really consider the issue. More people were stepping through the doors and shaking off their umbrellas, and I rushed to greet them.

I'd shown a few more of the guests to their seats and was crossing through a shadowed corner when Ray caught up to me. I saw him coming, and knew I should heed Nathaniel's order and brush him off. But Mrs. Brant was looking the other way, and the dim candlelight gave me confidence I probably shouldn't have had.

"Is everything okay?" he asked when he reached me.

"Everything's fine," I said, deciding after all to go with my wiser instincts.

"Really?" There was a challenge in that one word, an unspoken question, and I knew he'd wait for an answer.

I sighed. "No. Not really. But I can't stand here and talk about it."

"Is it something I've done?"

"What?" I turned toward him, surprised. "No. It's just Emeline's mother. She's blaming me for everything she can think of, and Nathaniel can't really do anything but go along with it."

As soon as I said the words, I wanted to take them back. Adding those concerns to Ray's already- overflowing list of to-dos and troubles was completely unprofessional at best and, at worst, putting more on a friend than he should be asked to handle. His eyebrows drew together.

"I can speak to them," he said, voice flat.

"No." I reached out and put a hand on his arm. "Please don't. That will just make things worse for both of us."

"Nathaniel, at least," he argued.

"Nathaniel is doing the best he can. Just let it go for now. Please. Tomorrow, all of this will be over with." I winced as I heard the words coming out of my mouth. "Sorry. Forget that last bit. What I meant was—"

Ray shook his head. "I know what you meant. And for you, it will be." He looked down at my hand where it rested on his arm, and lay his own over it. "You've been more help to me than I can tell you, Violet. Truly. Last night was... Well, thank you."

"You're welcome," I answered. "For whatever it was I did." I was reasonably sure he wasn't thanking me for kissing him.

More guests were arriving, and I heard someone call Ray's name. I quickly stepped back, clutching my seating chart on its clipboard to my chest like a shield. "I need to get back to work."

"Of course," Ray said.

I couldn't read the look on his face as I turned away and hurried back toward the door. Maybe it was disappointment. Maybe longing. I shoved the image of his eyes following me out of my thoughts and gave my full attention to seating.

Here were all the aunts and uncles and cousins Ray had told me stories about over the seating cards. It made me feel sorry all over again for Emeline, who had no one except her mother and her bridesmaids. It made me wonder who those girls were, how she'd come to choose them to be there for what was supposed to be the most important day of her life.

As I seated another group, Nathaniel returned with Emeline and Shannon. I was surprised to see that Emeline, wearing a Tiffany-blue dress that seemed to have been chosen to complement Shannon's seafoam green, was laughing as she entered, arm-in-arm with her maid of honor, their heads bent conspiratorially close together.

I couldn't recall if I had seen her smile like that before, lighting up her face all the way to her eyes. I didn't think I had. Her still-damp hair was pinned into a neat twist with silver and pearl combs. She looked, I thought, better in that than she had in the swirl of color she'd been wearing before, though it had likely looked different dry. Or maybe she just looked better when she smiled.

Definitely better when she smiled, I decided, as her mother rose from her chair with all the warmth of a statue come to life and crossed the room to pull her away from Shannon, hissing something in her ear. Emeline's smile faltered and fell apart, Shannon's dying with it. The bride-to-be retorted something I couldn't hear, her chin lifting. Mrs. Brant gestured to the closest table, a flick of her wrist indicating, I realized, the flower arrangements. It struck me abruptly that the dress she'd been wearing when they were caught in the rain must have been carefully chosen to match them, and the one she was currently wearing didn't. Was Mrs. Brant truly that Type A?

"Wow," a voice said at my back. "You look amazing. Much better in this than in the business chic you were rocking before."

I turned, and found James standing behind me. Without so much as a by-your-leave he caught me by the hand and spun me in a circle, whistling low and impressed. A blush I could have sworn started down at my toes heated my face all the way to the hairline. It had been a while since anyone had spent so much time scrutinizing me in a dress. Especially this dress.

"Thank you," I managed. "I—"

There was a sudden crash and boom of thunder and a brilliant flash of light. I jumped, and heard several gasps. The lights along the edges of the room and spilling from the hall down toward the kitchen flickered once, twice, and then went out entirely. There was a moment of stunned silence, and then the noise level in the room rose sharply.

Where was Nathaniel? I took a step and nearly stumbled. James caught my arm, pulling me against him.

"Stand still," he advised. "At least until your eyes adjust."

"The storm must have really picked up."

"Ray thought it would, at least going by what the guys at the terminal said. But I'm not sure they were expecting this."

"If I could have your attention, please." I recognized Bartholomew's voice, stern and commanding, coming from the front of the room. My eyes had adjusted enough that I could see him, too, in the light from the candles, though the dim illumination didn't offer much detail.

"Everyone remain where you are," Bartholomew said. "The staff will be bringing lanterns out in a moment for the buffet and such. And for those of you, like me, whose eyes aren't what they used to be."

There was a trickle of laughter and the waitresses appeared, each carrying battery-operated lanterns. They made a strangely eerie procession line through the room, setting the lights around the buffet and on some of the tables.

"Those of you still standing, please take a seat. There's no reason for us not to enjoy this wonderful dinner."

The guests standing moved to sit down, taking the closest available seats. So much for the seating chart I still held in my hands.

"Come on. You're with me." James still had his arm around my waist, and he pulled me with him toward the head table.

I pulled back, making him turn around. "Oh, no. I can't. I'm not a guest. And Nathaniel—"

"You're my guest," James said. "Come on."

And that was how I ended up sitting at the head table, between James and another groomsman, whose name I didn't catch in the exited buzz of family and friends that rose around me. I was going to give James approximately three minutes before I went to find Nathaniel.

"Why is there an empty chair?" I asked. I had to repeat myself before James actually heard me. He leaned over, his breath stirring the tendrils of hair that curled against my cheeks.

"Mike is a little busy tonight." James pointed toward the other end of the table, where there was also an empty chair on the bridesmaids' side.

"Oh." I blinked at the empty seat. "I see." I wondered if anyone had noticed earlier, or if anyone would now that the lights were out. But of course Nathaniel would. And Mrs. Brant, too. Emeline, I thought, would also know, but I wasn't certain she would care.

I was surprised that I hadn't seen Nathaniel yet. I tapped the ear piece I still wore, but there was nothing from it. The power going out shouldn't have affected the device, but maybe the storm was causing interference. I had a hard time believing Nathaniel didn't have something for me to do in all the chaos.

"I should go," I said, moving to rise.

"Or you could stay."

"I really can't." I gave him a smile to soothe the sting of the words. "I'm sure I'm going to be summoned any second."

As though mentioning him had been a summons, Nathaniel appeared along the room's edge. He crooked a finger at me, and I hurried across to where he stood.

"What on earth were you doing?" he demanded in a hiss as soon as I was close enough that the rest of the room wouldn't hear him.

"The best man wanted to talk to me." I glanced back toward the head table, where Emeline was leaning over to say something to Shannon. Ray caught my eye and gave me a tiny smile. James waved.

"The best man isn't paying the bill," Nathaniel snapped. "And we need to make sure this whole thing doesn't fall apart."

Bartholomew moved past us and Nathaniel fell briefly silent. The older man took up a place behind Ray and Emeline, Champagne flute in his hand. The servers were moving quietly through the room, filling everyone else's.

"We had planned a buffet service," he said first. "But with the lights out, I feel as though it's a bit risky for everyone to be walking around with plates of food. So our servers will be coming 'round to your tables instead and taking your orders. And now..." He smiled. "Let us all raise our glasses to Emeline and Ray. May this be the only storm on their horizon, and may all their future days be fair."

He raised his glass and others around the room lifted with it, gleaming in the candlelight. I saw, with some amusement, that in all the confusion Mrs. Brant had ended up at the same table with Ione and Drew. Exactly the place she didn't want to sit. It made the whole rearrangement of the seating chart—and all the work I'd done because of it—moot, but it was almost worth it to see the pinched look on her face.

"What do you need me to do?" I asked Nathaniel as the staff began moving efficiently between the tables.

"What I need you to do," Nathaniel said, "for a start, is to focus more on your job than on the eligible bachelor population of the island."

I turned sharply to look at him but he was already walking away down the hall, and I hurried after. He stopped in a shadowed alcove just short of the kitchen.

"I have tried to be understanding." He crossed his arms over his chest and looked down at me. "This is your first job in wedding planning, and there have been several unforeseen disasters, but as I'm sure you know there's no such thing as an event that runs smoothly. So even those are only so much of an excuse."

"Have I failed at my job somewhere?" I asked.

"Failed is a strong word. But you've certainly pushed the boundaries more than a few times." He sighed. "Tell me something, Violet. Are you just here to look for a rich husband?"

"What?" I stared at him. "Of course I'm not!"

"Then why are you so willing to risk your job hanging around them?"

I wanted to protest. But as I thought back over my time on the island, I couldn't find a defense. Nathaniel was right. I'd done my job, but only to the bare minimum. How many times had I been distracted by Ray and late to a destination? Frankly, Nathaniel had been shockingly understanding.

I took a deep breath. "I'm sorry, Nathaniel. I...I let myself get caught up. But this job *is* important to me. I promise. I'll do better from here on out."

Nathaniel gave me a long, searching look.

"See that you do," he said finally. "Now go and meet Andi at the main doors and find out where they're at with the generators."

I nodded and went.

Chapter Thirteen

I'd confirmed with Andi that the generators were going to be up and running shortly and was headed for an obscure corner of the villa under Nathaniel's orders, when I nearly ran directly into Emeline. She stopped, as shocked as I was, and we stared at each other in the glow of the lanterns that had been set out to make the hallways passable.

Last time we'd had an unexpected meeting she had been nothing but gracious. But the last time we'd had an unexpected meeting she hadn't seen me standing at a less-than-professional distance from her fiancé.

"Can I do anything for you, Emeline?" I asked, a little wary.

"No." Emeline swayed a little, and I wondered how much she'd had to drink. "No," she repeated.

"Are you okay?"

"Am I?" Emeline laughed without any mirth in it. "I mean, you'd think I would be having a wonderful time, right? I'm getting married to a wonderful man in the morning, on a private island, in a dress that cost more than most people's monthly salaries. It's a fairytale. Every girl's dream."

She pressed a hand to her mouth, her eyes welling up with tears, and I took a step forward. Not sure what to say, but unable to stand there and offer no comfort at all.

"I know you probably think I'm completely obnoxious," she went on before I could reach out. "I've been more than a little bridezilla about the whole thing. With the dress. But it's just that—" She paused, raising a glass of wine I hadn't realized she was carrying to her lips and tipping it back for a long swallow. "It's the only thing about this whole mess I have any control over. My mother picked the colors, the menu. The damn groom."

Her mouth shut abruptly, and she stood looking at me with wide eyes. Overhead, the lights flickered and came to life, leaving us both blinking against the sudden brightness. I thought, in the moment of silence, that I really needed to either stop members of the immediate family from using me as an impromptu therapist or figure out to be an actually useful one, because this was getting ridiculous.

"You don't want to marry Ray," I said. It wasn't really a question.

"I don't know," Emeline said, voice catching. "I thought I did." She took another drink of wine. "I do like him, you know. He's a good man. He really is. You know that." Her smile was lopsided and self-deprecating. "I've seen the way you look at him. And if it were up to me..."

She shook her head. "I'm sorry you can't have him, Violet. That is your name, right? Violet?"

I nodded mutely.

"Oh. Good. I'm terrible with names." She smiled again, but it trembled, and she looked down at the wine glass in her hand, her expression twisted into something aching. "I thought I could love him. I really did."

"I don't understand," I admitted.

"No," she said. "You wouldn't. How could you?" But she didn't sound arrogant, just near tears. "It would have made my mother happy, though. Finally. Maybe. Or, it will make her happy. She doesn't really care if I'm in love with Ray, as long as I marry him."

Tentatively I reached out, settling a hand on her shoulder. Emeline looked up at me. Then she reached up and lay her hand over it, holding tight.

"People still have arranged marriages," she said, more like she was trying to convince herself of something than like she was talking to me. "And they do just fine, right?"

"Why don't you just do what will make you happy?" I asked finally, unable to keep the question back any more.

Emeline sighed. "Because it doesn't work like that."

"I know your mother is important to you, but if she cares that little about your happiness why should you have to give so much concern to hers? No one should have to give up the chance to be with someone they love, Emeline. *Really* love."

She stared at me, tears spilling over.

"What if you forgot whatever agenda your mother is working toward and—"

Emeline's eyes widened too late. A hand closed around my shoulder, hauling me away from her, and I turned to look up at an irate Vivien Brant.

"That is *it*." Her words were practically a snarl. "I've put up with you because Nathaniel came highly recommended and I was willing to trust his judgment, but I have had enough of you sticking your nose where it doesn't belong."

"Mother..." Emeline said. And then again, more urgently, "Mother!"

Vivien was too busy dragging me down the hallway to listen. I stumbled after her on much shorter legs, dreading the moment that she would pull me out into the main room and the judging weight of all those eyes would turn and settle on my shoulders. It was almost a blessing that we met Nathaniel first.

His eyebrows snapped upward as he took in the sight of Mrs. Brant with her hand locked around my wrist. I saw his gaze go past us, to Emeline, who probably still looked as shell-shocked as I felt.

"Emeline," he said slowly. "Has something happened?"

"I'll tell you what's happened," Mrs. Brant snapped, cutting off her daughter's timid attempt at speaking almost before it started. "This girl has been sniffing around Ray since the moment she set foot on the island and I'm finally fed up with it."

"Do you think so?" Nathaniel, unlike me, was a consummate actor. "I know she's been a bit enamored, but Ray is a good-looking man. You can hardly blame a girl for a little admiration."

Mrs. Brant shook me like an ill-behaved dog. "It's more than that and you know it, Nathaniel."

Nathaniel took a deep breath and slowly let it out again. I saw the shift in his face before he spoke, and I knew where it was going. Knew there was nothing I could do to stop it. A reputation for eccentricity could only take him so far.

"You're right, of course, Vivien." The look he gave me said he'd warned me to keep out of it, and out of Mrs. Brant's way. I gave him the tiniest nod I could manage. Maybe I had brought it on myself, but I couldn't be sorry for what I'd said to Emeline. It wasn't fair to her, or to Ray, to force them into a marriage where neither one would be happy.

"She was just trying to comfort me," Emeline broke in. "There's no need for all this."

Her mother rounded on her. "She was trying to get you out of the way. She's a gold-digging little snake."

I yanked my wrist out of Mrs. Brant's hold. If I'd already lost my job, I wasn't going to stand there and take that without a word.

"You're just trying to get rid of me because I refuse to go around pretending I don't see what a farce this is."

"Violet!"

Mrs. Brant's eyes narrowed. "You think I don't see what you are? Hanging all over my son-in-law and stringing his best man along in your spare time? James Bradshaw is worth almost as much as Ray. You'd have quite a tidy little life if you snagged him, wouldn't you? I'm sure he's just what your mother told you to hook your claws into."

I felt my face burn hot. "As though you have any right to make up nonsense about my mother when you're practically dragging your daughter to the altar," I snapped. "It's obvious she's miserable, but you don't care as long as you get what you want. At least my mother sees me as more than a chess piece."

I spun on my heel, took three long strides down the hall, and then turned back. Emeline was wide-eyed and open-mouthed behind her mother. Nathaniel looked caught between horror and shocked delight. Vivien Brant was absolutely white with fury.

"And for the record? The reason Ray and James like me is that I'm a genuine, open person, and not a narcissistic manipulator grasping at any scrap of money or status I can get my hands on."

Mrs. Brant sputtered something behind me, no doubt involving threats to make sure I never worked in event planning again, but I'd had enough of her. I slipped out through a side door instead of heading through the main dining room. My only thought was to get to my cart and from there to my room. The fallout could wait until morning. Ray's family probably wouldn't want the hassle of Vivien figuring out they'd let me hitch a ride off the island, but maybe James would be willing to help. At the worst, Bartholomew would surely see that I was able to get back to the mainland.

The rain was coming down in sheets as I stalked out into the night, some of it blowing sideways. My dress was instantly soaked, clinging to me and wrapping around my legs. The heels were next to worthless in the wet grass and I took them off, running barefoot to my cart.

I sat on the wet seat, reaching for the key. It took a minute of fumbling to realize that it wasn't there, and another to realize where it must be. Nathaniel had used the cart. I sat back, blowing out a sigh. There were other carts lined up along the drive, and I briefly considered taking one, but that would mean someone else had to walk in the rain.

But what was I supposed to do? I couldn't very well go crawling back in, soaked and shivering, for Vivien Brant to mock. But far better slipping back into the villa and trying to find an out of the way corner than waiting in the rain for them to come out and find me huddled in the cart. I was climbing out when I heard someone call my name.

Peering through the rain, I caught sight of a figure waving at me from the porch. My heart jumped a little, hoping it might be Ray or James. But then I realized that the figure in the rain slicker was too narrow in the shoulders to be either of them. It was Andi.

"Here, Violet. Come with me."

She held out another raincoat and helped me shrug into it. It was a little large, falling nearly to my knees, the sleeves swallowing up my hands. But it was protection against the rain and the wind.

"What are you doing out here?" I pushed at the wet hair clinging to my face and looked up at her, grateful for the shelter of the porch.

"I came from the terminal," Andi said, ushering me along the veranda and down the steps to a cart that must have been hers. "I needed to talk to Mr. Court. The storm has taken out all our communications."

"Are we in any danger?" I asked, sliding into the vehicle.

"We're out of the direct path of the storm. This is about as bad as it's going to get. But the lightning must have hit something important, and we can't go check until morning." She turned the cart toward the path that would take us to my little villa at the end of the island. "It would be a pretty minor inconvenience if it weren't for the wedding."

"I can't imagine Vivien Brant envisioned her daughter getting married in the dark during a tropical storm."

Andi laughed, the sound doing more to warm me than the clammy slicker could. "Some couples specifically ask to be married by candlelight, you know. And the generators are already back up, so it will hardly be dark either way. They may not be able to have the beach wedding Emeline hoped for, which is a shame. But they'll have a wedding either way."

Emeline had wanted the beach wedding. I felt for her all over again. She'd managed to wrest control from her mother in so few things, and now she was losing even that. But the villa had looked lovely in the flickering light after the power went out, and the alternate space for the ceremony was smaller. More intimate. With enough candles, it would be gorgeous. If she couldn't have what she wanted, maybe she would at least get something beautiful.

The headlights of the cart barely cut through the rain, but I trusted that Andi knew where she was going. And she did, parking practically at the foot of the steps. I slid out of the cart, turning back to her.

"Thank you. For everything, Andi." I smiled, even though I wasn't sure she could see it. "You've helped me so much, and I really appreciate it."

She reached out, resting a hand on my shoulder. "My pleasure, Violet. Truly. I know you've had a rough go of it here."

"You don't know the half of it," I sighed. "I got fired tonight, because Mrs. Brant caught me asking Emeline why she was going through with something she so clearly doesn't want to do. She threw a fit. Nathaniel didn't really have a choice."

Andi was polite enough not to point out that I never should have said anything of the sort to Emeline if I really valued my job. The rain was lashing against the back of my slicker and running down my legs. I clutched the slick ankle straps of my heels and turned to go.

"Listen," Andi said behind me, "if you're ever interested in working here, don't hesitate to talk to Mr. Court."

I turned to look over my shoulder, and Andi went on. "He's always looking for hard-working people, and I know he's taken a liking to you. He won't balk at a bit of honesty in others' best interest either."

I stared at her. "Really?"

She smiled. "Really. But we can talk about that tomorrow. For now, you'd better get yourself inside and out of those soaked clothes." She reached into the back seat and handed one of the battery-operated lanterns to me. "Take this, too. The generators are only for the main house."

I ran up the steps, bare feet slapping against the wet wood and hair clinging to my cheeks. Down at the bottom Andi waited, the lights of the cart shining on the door, until I was inside. Then she turned the cart around. With her, much of the light was gone. Left alone, I sat in my little circle of lantern glow and felt peace settle over me for the first time in hours.

Chapter Fourteen

After everything that had happened, my little room felt like heaven. It was cozy and warm, the wind and rain distant noises. I dropped the raincoat on the tile floor by the door and stripped out of Lydia's dress, hanging it on the back of the bathroom door, my wet lingerie dumped unceremoniously in the sink.

Under the warm water of the shower, I finally felt like I could breathe. I'd pulled the pins out of my hair and let the water run through it and down my back, washing away the chill of the storm and the irritation that had buzzed like static on my skin. I scrubbed the makeup off my face, then tipped my face up into the stream to rinse it. The white noise of the water falling, and the rain beyond that, emptied my head of every thought. When I finally turned off the water, I felt cleansed of more than just the physical dust of the day.

Bundled up in my pajamas and a fluffy robe I made a detour to the tiny kitchen, grabbing a bottle of wine and a glass. I felt like I deserved it. Then I headed to the bed, slipped off the robe, pulled back the covers, and crawled between the sheets. Outside the wind was howling, but I was safe and warm in the sturdy little villa. Sure, I was technically jobless and semi-stranded, but at least I had a place to stay the night. The curtains around the bed made it feel like its own little world, sheltered from anything beyond my walls.

Besides, there was nothing I could do about the job situation at the moment. I wrestled the cork out of the bottle and poured myself a generous glass of pale amber wine. It was fruity and sweet, and pooled

HE LOVES ME NOT 119

warmth in my stomach, slowing leeching the last of the tension from my muscles.

On the bedside table the lantern cast a soft glow across the bed, and I sat in its circle of light and thought about what had happened. I'd finally decided to speak up about the farce they were trying to pass off as a wedding, and it had cost me my job. Or I'd lost my temper. The trouble was, the chance at working for Nathaniel really had been the opportunity of a lifetime. Without it, I was stuck working my way up the ranks the slow way. Or not at all. No doubt Vivien Brant would do her very best to see that I never got another job in the event industry again. I'd be lucky if I was allowed to be a catering waiter. I thought about calling Lydia and letting her know, just to hear someone's voice, to know I wasn't the only person who cared. But Lydia would only worry, and there was nothing she could do from across an ocean anyway. I'd just have to look for something when I got back.

Or maybe I'd take Andi's suggestion and speak with Bartholomew. There was no harm in asking, at least. And working indefinitely in paradise didn't sound so bad, even with the occasional tropical storm. Anything after the Rose-Brant wedding would be a breeze. In my heart of hearts, though, I couldn't see myself leaving my family or Lydia so far behind. And what about Irving? He probably wouldn't be pleased with relocation to the hot and humid tropics.

After a while, though, I wasn't thinking so much about the job. The wine had brought with it a pleasant haziness, and for the moment I was still on a private island paradise with no further obligations. Maybe the storm would clear up in time for a bit of a swim in the morning. Or maybe... I still had one dress in my luggage. It wasn't as nice as the one I'd borrowed from Lydia, but with the heels and a little makeup it might be presentable. Maybe, even though I was no longer the wedding planner's assistant, I'd attend the wedding after all.

The wind had settled into the background, but I heard something banging rhythmically against the wall. I sat up and listened, trying to figure out the source of the noise. My heart beat a little faster. What if it wasn't just the wind? I was all alone out here. I peered around the curtain and was surprised to see a light out on the patio, feebly spilling through across the floor of my room.

I clambered out of bed, stumbling through the semi-darkness to the French doors. There was a pool of yellow light on the patio, and in the middle of that light stood Ray. I threw open the doors. The wind whipped at my hair and tugged at my nightgown, rain pelting against my bare arms and legs, sending shivers through me. I grabbed his arm, pulling him inside.

"Ray! What are you doing? You're soaked."

Ray stood barefoot just inside the doors, and dripped a puddle on the wood floor. I ducked into the bathroom and grabbed one of the remaining bath towels.

"Here." I held it out to him and he looked at it, and then down at his soaking wet clothes, and we both burst out laughing.

"I'm not really sure where to start."

"Start at the top, I guess? Wait..." I ran to the bed, grabbed the robe, and held it out to him. "You can change in there." I pointed to the bathroom.

He took the towel and the robe, along with his lantern. His face was cast in eerie shadows and he paused before shutting the door, his expression unreadable.

I closed my eyes, drawing in a deep breath. My mind was starting to work again and I wondered what the heck he was doing here, in the middle of a huge storm, barefoot and soaking wet. That question probably wasn't the best one to lead with.

"Do you want some wine?" I called through the door instead. "I just opened a bottle."

There was a muffled sound that I took for yes. I grabbed a second glass from the kitchen and filled it, topping mine off as well. And then I glanced around my little space. There wasn't much for seating, other than the bed and a tiny table with two chairs, and I had a brief moment of panic.

Before I could get too wound up in the potential impropriety of sitting on the bed with someone's fiancé, Ray opened the bathroom door and stepped out. My thoughts fractured and fell apart.

While the robe I'd given him had been big and fluffy on me, on Ray's much larger and taller frame it hugged his body, the hem just above his knees. He'd tied the sash around his waist, but the neck of the robe was open. I tried hard not to stare, but his smooth skin and broad chest were almost too much. Biting my lip to keep in something that felt like a whimper I turned away, fumbling for the glass of wine I'd poured for him.

"Here." I held out the glass and he took it, his eyes on me. My nightgown was damp from standing in the open doorway and I could feel a breeze snaking along the floor, chilling my feet. I wrapped my arms around myself and watched him take a swallow from the glass.

"This is good," he said, glancing down with something like surprise. "Bartholomew must have had Andi stock your room with some of the nice stuff."

I nodded, not trusting my voice. The little moment dragged on for the space of a heartbeat, and then another. Finally, I shook myself loose from my trance. As strange as the circumstances might be, we couldn't just stand in the middle of the room drinking wine all night.

"I'd offer you a chair," I said, glancing around the room like one might appear. "But..." I rubbed my upper arms with my hands, trying to soothe the goosebumps rising there.

His eyebrows drew together. "You're shivering," he said. "Here." He took my hand, leading me to the bed. It was the place I most wanted to be, and the very last place I wanted to go. Setting his glass next to mine on the bedside table, he whisked back the curtain and drew the blankets down. "Get in. Cover up. You'll catch a cold." The tiny furrow between his eyebrows deepened, oddly familiar.

It hit me where I'd seen that look. I giggled. He looked at me like he thought I might be getting hysterical.

"What's so funny?"

"Nothing. It's just— You look like your grandmother. She gets that same little line between her eyebrows."

"Under the covers," Ray said again, coaxingly.

He was a little bit irresistible. I sat down, scooting up against the head of the bed, and tucked my legs beneath me. Ray reached down and pulled the blankets up, then handed me my glass.

"This will take the chill off." He didn't sit on the bed, but paced across the room. It didn't take him very far away. The room, which had seemed cozy with one person, seemed small with two.

"Ray." He turned as I spoke, standing in the shadows at the foot of the bed.

"Why are you here?" I asked, because the question was eating away at me. "There's a huge storm outside. The lights are out..."

"Emeline told me what happened, and I wanted to apologize. And to see how you're doing."

"That's really thoughtful of you, but I'm doing just fine."

"You got fired," Ray retorted.

I was glad for the dim light in the room. Glad that he was still in the shadows. I didn't know if Emeline had told him that her mother had accused me of being a gold-digger. Didn't know if I could bring myself to ask what he knew.

"I've been fired before," I said. "And things turned out just fine."

It might mean a few lean weeks or month, a lot of ramen, but I would get by. And Lydia wasn't going to kick me out of the apartment if I couldn't pay rent for a month.

"It wasn't my fault before."

"It wasn't your fault this time. It was Emeline's mother. She..."

Ray sighed, running a hand through his damp hair. "I know. Emeline didn't really give me any details. Just told me that she insisted on Nathaniel firing you. But I can guess some of what happened."

Well, at least he hadn't heard the worst part.

"Did you see where she ended up sitting?" he asked, brightening a little.

I laughed. "Yeah. I did. The absolute last place she wanted to be seated."

"Served her right," Ray said. His grin faded. He came around the end of the bed, leaning against the corner post. Our eyes met, and in that instant something passed between us, a tiny spark of heat, a connection. I saw more pain behind Ray's eyes than I could have imagined. Tears instantly welled in my eyes and I blinked them away.

"Ray? What else? Something's not right." I leaned forward. "Tell me."

He sat on the end of the bed and I was conscious of his weight dipping the mattress. My heart started beating in a stuttering little staccato rhythm, and equal parts fear and anticipation raced through me.

Where he sat, his eyes on the floor, Ray's face was lit by the golden glow of the lantern. I looked at his profile. The long, straight nose. The strong jaw. His lashes rested in a soft curve against his cheek. He was so beautiful. I swallowed hard, and waited for him to speak.

"It's been one obstacle after another with this wedding. I'm starting to wonder if it's some kind of sign."

It would be easier on us both if I told him that it was just the way things went. That there was no such thing as an event without at least one disaster. No battle plan ever survives contact with the enemy. I'd heard that somewhere and thought it very applicable. But telling him that would be a lie.

He went on before I could speak. "I keep telling myself it will be different once we're married and back in New York, when things settle into a routine. I'll go back to work and she'll... go on volunteering with the charity, I guess. But that's only so much diversion, and I'm not really sure she's cut out to be a housewife. Maybe I can talk her into going back to school. I think she's always wanted to, from some of the things she's said, but her mother didn't like the idea."

"Her mother doesn't like a lot of things." The only things she did like, I was starting to see, were Ray's money and social status.

"That's one of the reasons I want to get Emeline out of there."

"I know. You told me. But, Ray..." I'd already lost my job. What else did I have to lose. "Is it worth it?"

He stared down at his hands. "I don't know," he admitted.

I pushed the blankest aside, crawling across the small distance between us, and knelt beside him. I slid a hand into his hair and stroked gently. "I'll ask you what I asked Emeline. Why not forget what her mother wants and do what's best for you?"

Ray still wouldn't look at me. I put a hand on his shoulder and tugged, turned him so that he finally raised his eyes to mine.

"It's not just her mother," he said hoarsely.

I had kind of gathered that. James had mentioned pressure from his parents, and his grandmother had mentioned duty. I thought, for the first time, about the comment she'd made regarding a company merger. I'd been more caught up at the time in what Ray felt, or didn't feel, for Emeline than anything to do with other factors.

"Then what is it?" I asked, because I wanted him to tell me outright.

His shoulders slumped. "Honestly? The whole thing is a business deal. Emeline and I are just the pieces our parents are moving on the board."

Chapter Fifteen

It wasn't some kind of shocking secret. Looking back, it was honestly more surprising that I hadn't picked up Ione's meaning immediately. But I'd relegated the off-hand mention to a footnote. Just one of the reasons Ray had stuck around long enough to start believing he had to save Emeline. It hadn't occurred to me that a company merger could be the entire reason for a marriage in the modern era.

"When Vivien's husband died," Ray said, "he left Vivien a number of holdings. Most of them were fairly modest. Enough to support her and Emeline in the lifestyle they were accustomed to. But one of the companies she owns is part of the supply chain to one of my parents' larger investments. They want it, and she's more than happy to give it to them, in exchange for my last name and the social boost of marriage into an old New England family." He laughed once, sharply. "That, and the promise of more money than even she needs to maintain appearances."

I frowned at him. "Aren't they already wealthy?"

"Vivien puts on a lot of airs and show, but their assets are in the hundreds of thousands. Ours are in the multi-millions. With my family's money, she can actually be what she passes herself off as."

"And your parents... want a company?" I still couldn't wrap my head around it.

"It's the missing link. With it, they're well on their way to an incredibly lucrative monopoly. Although, of course, they won't call it that." Ray shrugged. "They're pretty set on the acquisition."

"So set on it they would trap their son in a marriage he doesn't want?" Anger rose hot in my chest. "They're rich enough to be hobnobbing around with people who *own their own islands*. What do they even need more money for?"

When Ray turned to look at me, he was wearing a crooked half-smile that did nothing to disguise the pain behind his eyes. "What do any of the people in our tax bracket need more money for?"

"I can't imagine anyone raised by your grandparents would care so much about a bank account."

"It's mostly my father's influence." Ray's voice was tight. "You haven't met his parents, but they have a lot more in common with Vivien Brant than with Grandpa Drew and Grandma Ione."

"So that explains why *they* go along with it." I met his eyes, so deep a blue in the lantern-light. "But why do you?"

Ray's gaze dropped. Silent, he stared down at his hands, folded in his lap. "Honestly?" He swallowed. "I'm afraid they'll cut me off if I don't."

The words reached my ears, but didn't register. I looked up at him incredulously. "What?"

"I don't mean they'll turn me out into the street," he said, raising his head enough to look at me from the corner of his eye. "My grandparents wouldn't let them anyway. But... I could lose their respect." *Lose their love.* He didn't say it, but the words hung in the air between us, filling the space with the ghost of their presence. "They're still my parents, Violet."

"I understand that." I lay a hand on his shoulder and he reached up to squeeze it tightly. "I'm not trying to cut you off from them, Ray. I'm just asking you to consider if it's worth a lifetime in a marriage you never wanted. Don't you think you're worth more than that?"

"It's hardly a lifetime." His voice was flat. "We just have to wait long enough that a divorce won't be a scandal."

I pulled back, staring at him. "You *what*?"

"The rules for this kind of thing are a little different than what you're used to," Ray said, eyebrows drawing together again. "It's not like two people in love and 'till death do us part' and all of that. It's just a business arrangement. At least these days they're easy enough to get out of when they've served their purpose." He tried on a self-deprecating smile. "A few decades ago, it really would have been a life sentence."

He reached for my shoulder, and I pulled away before he could make contact. Hurt flashed across his expression. I felt my stomach twist at the look but there were words rising up in my throat, and I didn't know if I'd be able to get them out if he was touching me. If I could feel the warmth of his skin against my own.

"Do you even hear yourself? 'A life sentence'? Is that all marriage is to you?" He opened his mouth, but I rushed on. "It can't just be a business transaction, Ray. It has to mean something, or what's the point of it?"

"Marriage has been a business transaction for a long time," Ray said, meeting my eyes. His expression was empty.

"And where did that get us?" I retorted. "If marriage is just a business transaction? If the two of you are just...just tokens on a board? You're *human*, Ray. You and Emeline both. And you deserve to be treated like people, with your own emotions and desires and lives ahead of you."

I forced out the next words before I could stop long enough to talk myself out of saying them. "I don't think we should be here like this. Together." I couldn't meet his eyes. "You should go back to your villa."

Still not looking at him, I levered myself upright. His hand closed gently around my arm before I could leave the bed behind, and despite my better judgment I went still under the touch, my breath catching.

"Is that what you really want?" he asked quietly behind me. "For me to leave?"

No. But that didn't mean it wasn't the right thing for him to do.

He tugged on my shoulder, turning me toward him. His eyes searched mine, his expression unreadable.

Or maybe it wasn't as unreadable as I wanted it to be. Maybe it was a look I didn't want to recognize. Because if I did, I'd have to face something I'd been hiding from myself. I'd have to face the fact that the harmless crush I had on Ray was something else, something far deeper. I'd have to face that I wanted him. And that he wanted me.

I leaned forward and so did he. Our lips met. There was a moment, so brief it was already passing before I even caught it, when I wondered if I should stop. But from Ray there was only certainty, no hesitation at all.

He turned, pushing me down against the mattress, his lips against mine, claiming my mouth quickly, fiercely. I'd never been kissed like that. So hungrily. It took me by surprise. But despite the weight of him pressing me to the bed, despite the need with which his lips devoured mine, his hands were tender against my face and I felt free and light and his equal.

I ran my hands over his cheeks, up through his hair, holding him to me as I strained up against the heat of his body. I needed more of him. More of his lips, his mouth. My heart thumped so loudly I could feel it in my fingertips, and I was sure he could hear it.

When we broke apart, we were both breathless. Ray looked down at me, his eyes brilliantly blue. I felt my heartbeat falter all over again.

"Violet," he whispered, and the sound of my name on his lips, barely heard above the noise of the rain on the roof, ignited the warmth from the wine and sent tendrils of heat through my body. I arched my back, eager for more contact.

Ray buried his head against my shoulder, his body moving against me in counterpoint to my movements, slow and powerful and wonderful. The brush of his mouth behind my ear had me moaning softly. I ran my hands over his shoulders and down his back, digging my fingers into the thick fabric of the robe, aching to touch him, skin to skin.

The heat in me grew, my desire for Ray hitting me hard, low, almost knocking the breath out of me. I wanted to be out of my damp nightgown, wanted him out of the robe, and I wiggled beneath him. He lifted his head, eyes locked with mine, reading my thoughts in the movement of my body.

Ray rose above me, and with eager fingers I undid the sash on the robe. With graceful movements he was out of the garment, tossing it aside. All that was left between us was the thin fabric of my nightgown.

One hand slid down my leg, cupping my thigh for a moment before searching for the hem of my gown. With infinite slowness he began tugging the fabric up my leg, his eyes never leaving mine. I was twitching in anticipation, the hard contours of his body pressing against me.

As his fingers moved higher, taking the gown up over my thigh and then my hip, his eyes watched me, wanting dark in them. He smiled and leaned down, kissing me slow and deep, teasing me with his tongue against my lips as his fingers teased against my skin.

I had his face in my hands, the subtle prickle along his jawline mesmerizing to my fingers. My body was moving on its own now, trying to slide out of the gown, wiggling and twisting. I felt his lips curving into a lazy smile and I opened my eyes, pulling away.

"You think this is funny?" I demanded even as I returned the smile, stretching my arms over my head, the invitation clear, paving the way for the gown to be history.

"I'm enjoying myself," Ray answered. "Like Christmas. Unwrapping is half the fun. I don't rip my paper apart. I pull it off nice and slow."

Damn, I hoped not. "I'm a paper shredder. I've been known to tear the bows off with my teeth."

Ray threw his head back and laughed. "Okay. Okay. I don't want bite marks." He rose up again, kneeling between my legs, the nightgown held in both hands. My eyes slid over his form, smooth muscle and summer-tan skin gilded in the lamplight. The nightgown slid over my head, and for a moment the view cut off. I raised my shoulders to free the last of the fabric from beneath me.

"You almost took my breath away in that dress," he said, eyes roaming over my body. "It was such an improvement over that jacket. But this..." He met my eyes then leaned down, resting his elbows alongside my body. "You're beautiful, Violet. Perfect."

We kissed then, for a long time, bodies pressed together. There was no mistaking either of our intentions then, or where this was headed.

The heat and desire between us finally reached the boiling point, where kissing and touching, hands exploring and moving, weren't enough. It seemed to hit us both at the same time and suddenly I had my legs wrapped around Ray, and he was there, ready. And I was ready for him.

That first touch of him against me, as he held my face in his hands, watching me, took my breath away. And then it intensified as he slowly slid into me, as he filled me in a way I'd never known before.

"Damn, Violet..." His eyes were closed, lips parted, his body taut, holding us on the edge of this experience. I wanted more, but watching his face, feeling every subtle movement of his body, held me enraptured.

I touched his face and he opened his eyes, looking down at me with a heavy-lidded gaze. Beneath him I shifted my hips slightly, slowly, just enough to feel him moving inside me. He responded, pressing himself deeper, pulling back as I shifted away, surging forward again to meet the rise of my hips.

"Ray," I gasped.

"Later," he answered, pressing a finger to my lips.

I lost track of time, and pretty everything else. I was aware, dimly, of the rain and wind, and occasional flashes of lightning. But it was distant, removed. All my focus was on Ray, on the fire he'd started, the fire that was now raging through me. And on our dance together, the beauty of how our bodies moved and twisted together, how seamlessly we fit together. How perfect this moment was.

Then all the swirling feelings that had been building inside of me reached a crescendo, and I hung there for long moments, aching to stay in this place, in this plateau of bliss with Ray. But there was no holding back now, for either of us.

And then everything seemed to explode. I cried out, clutching at Ray, writhing and bucking beneath him. Ray buried his head in my shoulder, his arms around me, holding me hard against him as release flooded through me. Then I felt him tense, every muscle in his body taut, waiting there for a moment, seeking his own release in my body. He rose above me, braced himself over me and then thrust hard and fast, and I knew he'd found it.

In that moment his face carried so much emotion, such an open vulnerability, that I was almost overwhelmed being there, watching him. His eyes met mine, a tenderness in them that warmed me all the way down to my still-curling toes.

Body still shuddering above me, Ray caressed my face. He lowered his head, gasping against my neck, and I held him close. The storm was still beating against the walls outside, but in the villa we were our own little island of calm.

We lay tangled in each other's arms and legs, our bodies damp with perspiration. Ray finally rolled onto his back, one hand on his chest and the other resting on my thigh.

"Violet," he said, voice hoarse in the aftermath.

I turned toward him in the glow of the lamps. He smiled, light filling his face, his eyes. I smiled back.

"Are you okay?" he asked gently. "Why are you crying?"

"Crying?" I hadn't realized I was. His fingertips traced the path of a tear down my cheek, brushing away the warmth I hadn't noticed until he pointed it out.

"It's fine," I said, because it was. "I just..."

His smile deepened. "Yeah," he said, leaning down to press his lips to my forehead. "I know."

He pulled me to him and I nestled against his chest, inhaling his scent. Wrapped in his arms, I felt warm and safe in a way I hadn't since before Evan. I gave myself over to the moment, closed my eyes, and was instantly asleep.

I WOKE TO RAY GENTLY shaking my shoulder.

I was curled on my side, my back against his chest. One of his arms was under the weight of my body, my fingers tangled with his.

"Hmm?" I grumbled, rolling over. He leaned up on an elbow, looking down at me.

"I need to go." His voice was soft, heavy with apology. "It's almost dawn."

"No." I closed my eyes again, willing it to be some other time. Some other place. Anywhere but here on the morning of his wedding. The wedding, I realized, he must have decided to go through with, even after the conversation we'd had the night before.

I shouldn't have expected anything else.

"Violet," Ray said. I felt a finger trace the curve of my jawline, stroking my lower lip. "I have to go."

I opened my eyes, blinking in the pale gray light of predawn, and looked up the face that become beloved in such a short time. "Are you sorry?" I asked, throat tight.

"Sorry? About what?" That little indent appeared between his eyebrows. "About us?" His kissed my forehead, lips lingering along my hairline, and the rest of his answer was muffled against my hair. "Never," he promised. "Don't ever think that I would be."

"But you have to go." The finality of my own words hit me in the chest like a fist. Tears welled up in my eyes, and when I closed them I felt the wet heat of them sliding down my cheeks.

"Don't. Violet." Ray's voice faltered. "Please. I don't regret this. What we had. But I have an obligation to Emeline. I can't just abandon her."

"I know." I nodded weakly. "And I know this was just..." One last fling, apparently.

"It was amazing," Ray finished. "*You're* amazing. And if I had the choice..."

This time it was my turn to finish. "But you don't." He'd already made his choice. "So you have to go."

Ray looked at me one last time. I searched his face, his eyes, and found the same longing there that I felt. But, as he'd already said, he had an obligation to Emeline. And that meant I had to let him go.

Chapter Sixteen

When Ray was gone, the door closing hard and final behind him, I cried myself into a fitful sleep. My mind knew there could be nothing more, but my heart didn't want to hear that. It wanted Ray.

I woke a second time to a bed that felt cold, the digital alarm clock on the nightstand still black and dead. The power was still out. I fumbled for my cell phone, glad to see it still had some battery left. It was just before eight in the morning.

Sinking back onto the pillows, I thought of the night before. And then I tried very hard not to think about the day to come. But images of Ray standing at the altar, waiting for Emeline, were stamped indelibly across my mind's eye.

The light spilling in through the gaps in the curtains was a pearly gray that suggested the sun hadn't yet made an appearance, but the sound of rain on the roof had stopped sometime in the hours after dawn. I could, I decided, lie there in bed feeling sorry for myself for the rest of the morning, or I could get up and go to the wedding. Watch Ray marry Emeline and see for myself that the brief moment we'd shared was truly over.

I sat up and swung my feet over the side of the bed. They landed on something soft, and I looked down to find that the robe Ray had been wearing was crumpled on the floor. I reached for it and buried my nose in the terry cloth, searching for any scent of Ray, but all I smelled was fabric and laundry soap. Heart aching, I slipped the robe on and headed into the bathroom.

My lingerie from the night before was still in the sink. I stood looking down at it. It was still damp. I couldn't pack it like that. Mechanically, I hung it over the shower rod to finish drying.

In the kitchen I made myself a mug of steaming black coffee, then I headed out to the patio. With the sun still hidden behind the clouds and the lingering chill of rain, the breeze was just cool enough to be refreshing. It, and the coffee, cleared some of the fog from my brain.

The wedding was scheduled to start at noon. While it had originally been planned to take place down on the beach, I doubted they would want to hold the ceremony outside in the gloomy weather. The building they'd set up as a secondary option was up near the main villa. My cart had been left behind in the storm, but there was plenty of time to walk.

I owed it to myself to be there. To put what had happened behind me. It didn't matter what it had meant to me, or to Ray. There was no future in it.

I dressed slowly, my mind preoccupied, thoughts tangled up in memories of Ray from the night before. I remembered, all too vividly, the way his hands had felt on my skin, the way his mouth had felt on mine. It was all I would ever have of him, and that knowledge tore a hole through my heart. I'd lost lovers before, ended relationships, but this was so much harder.

Maybe it was the intensity of the forbidden, the atmosphere of the island. Or maybe it was just that I couldn't stop thinking about him starting a life he might never be happy in. About him and Emeline both trapped by their parents' machinations.

When I was finally dressed I stood in front of the mirror, looking myself over. The second dress wasn't quite as formal as the first; I'd only intended to wear it on the plane ride home. It was a simple V-neck maxi dress, in a blue that almost matched the Caribbean Sea. Pretty, although not really suitable for a society wedding, but it would have to do. I had a lightweight cream-colored shawl in my luggage, and I draped it around my shoulders as I stepped out the door.

Despite the turmoil roiling in my chest, the walk was pleasant. Water still dripped from leaves and petals along the paths, but birds were singing and the air smelled clean and fresh. The sky was a silvery pewter that was surprisingly pretty.

There were several carts in front of the small building that was serving as the chapel, and a few guests lingered on the front steps. I hung back, waiting for them to go inside, hoping to slip in at the last minute and slide unnoticed into a bench at the back.

As I got closer I saw that Andi was standing at the door, dressed in a pale pink pantsuit that was very flattering on her. She saw me and her eyes went wide. Then she smiled and came down the steps to meet me.

"This is a pleasant surprise. You're not working, are you?" She cocked an inquisitive eyebrow at me.

"No, I..." I looked up toward the chapel.

"You're here for Ray," Andi said, not a question. "I've seen the way you two look at each other."

I winced. "Is it that obvious?"

"You light up when you see him. And the feeling isn't one-sided."

Tears pricked at my eyes and I blinked them back.

Andi's gentle hand settled on my shoulder. "Come and let me seat you."

I hesitated.

"Nathaniel and Vivien aren't in the chapel. They're with Emeline in the changing room. Neither of them will see you."

She hooked her arm through mine and led me inside. I stopped just inside the door, breath catching.

Candles were everywhere: on tall holders at the ends of the gleaming wooden pews, grouped in crystal holders on the window sills, amassed in out of the way corners. The light made the dark wood of the rafters and support beams glow and gilded the cream-colored walls. In contrast to the gray light outside the place seemed like something out of a storybook, the perfect space for a fairytale wedding.

Adding to that impression was the profusion of flowers, all of them white. They were tied to the ends of the pews with champagne-colored ribbons, hanging from the tall candle holders, dripping from every niche and nook. The scents of jasmine and freesia filled the room. Freesia, I thought, with a rush of painful amusement. That was ironic. But the effect was enchanting, and all an illusion.

Andi guided me to a seat in one of the pews at the back corner. There were several other people in the row, but they were seated together closer to the aisle, and none of them looked at me.

I'd just been seated when movement at the front of the room signaled the beginning of the proceedings. A door to the side opened, admitting Ray and James, both of them in suits a shade darker than the ribbons that bound the flowers and rose-colored waistcoats. No black in the tropics, it seemed. They took their places at the front of the chapel, hands clasped before them.

I craned my neck, trying to catch a glimpse of Ray's face, to read his expression. He looked somber, I thought, not eager. Not even accepting. Just weighted down. As I watched he fidgeted, rocking back and forth on his heels, and flexed the fingers of one hand against the other. Then James leaned over, whispered something in Ray's ear, and nodded in my direction.

I froze, heart in my throat. Ray's eyes lifted and met mine, and for an instant everything and everyone else in the room disappeared. I saw recognition, maybe even happiness, spark in his expression, his eyes lighting up. My heart surged, beating double-time—and then I remembered where I was. Ray, too, must have recalled in the same moment. Loss eclipsed the brief light. I couldn't do it, couldn't sit there and lose him all over again. I half-rose from my seat.

It was too late. Music began to play as I rose, and I sank back into the pew, wrapping myself closer in my shawl. Everyone turned as Mrs.

Brant began walking down the aisle, back stiff and eyes straight ahead. She took her seat in the front pew without ever turning her head to see me.

Ray's grandparents were next, walking in arm in arm. Then his parents. With everyone seated there was a moment of silence, like the deep breath before the plunge.

The bridal party began their sedate walk down the aisle, couples splitting at the end and taking their places to either side of the altar. They looked exquisite, the bridesmaids in gowns of champagne silk, with pink roses in their hair, the groomsmen pressed and polished.

Shannon, the maid of honor, walked alone. The pale silk seemed to glow against the brown of her skin. I wondered if Emeline had chosen the dresses because she knew just how stunning Shannon would look in that color. She reached her spot and turned, and the music stopped.

All heads were turned toward the back of the chapel. Except mine. I had my eyes fixed on Ray, and as the music swelled again and the guests rose in anticipation of Emeline's entrance I watched his face, wishing despite my own desire for him that I could see the joy that should have been on his face on his wedding day. But, of course, it wasn't there.

A murmur ran through the room as Emeline stepped into view. I turned, finally. She looked beautiful, ethereal, glowing in the candlelight. But it was as much a facade as the rest of the event. She walked alone, as her mother had, and I wondered why Mrs. Brant hadn't escorted her daughter down the aisle. Why there was no one there to give her away.

As she reached the end of the aisle Ray stepped forward, taking her arm, and they walked the last few steps together. Shannon stepped forward from her position and arranged the train of the dress, took the bouquet of pink and champagne roses from Emeline. She looked, I thought, like she was moving by rote, so expressionless I had to wonder what she was thinking beneath it. The whole thing was a play, everyone miming their way through their assigned parts and waiting for the farce to end.

The officiant began the ceremony, but I didn't hear the words. All my attention was focused on Ray and Emeline. The tension between them was palpable: Emeline as straight-backed as her mother, Ray's shoulders tight. For them, the wedding was just the beginning of the act.

As the officiant droned on, the cadence familiar from more than a few weddings, I finally dragged my eyes away from Ray. His parents sat, inches of space between them, eyes straight ahead, and I was struck by the similarity between them and Ray and Emeline. Why had they married, I wondered. Surely they hadn't been in the same situation. When had their relationship lost the love that must have once been there?

Ione and Drew, one pew back, were pressed close together. I was sure they were holding hands. I watched as Ione leaned toward Drew, her lips to his ear. He shook his head and she sighed, turning back to Ray and Emeline.

"Before our couple says their vows, we have a few formalities to go over." He smiled. "If anyone here," the officiant said, the words registering for the first time as I realized what part of the ceremony he had just hit, "knows a just cause as to why these two should not be joined in holy matrimony, let him speak now or forever hold his peace."

I opened my mouth, words forming, but they stayed frozen in my throat. I couldn't do that to Ray. Couldn't stop him from making his own choice. He was an adult, and he had that right. There was a rustle of movement from Drew and Ione, a brief whispered conversation. For an instant, I thought one of them might say something. My hands curled until I felt my own nails cut into my skin.

"Then by the power vested in me," the officiant went on, voice rising in anticipation of delivering the happy news that Ray and Emeline were man and wife. I blinked back tears. "I now pronounce you—"

"Stop."

The officiant faltered to silence, turning to look at Ray. His eyebrows lifted. "Excuse me?"

"I said stop." Ray glanced at Emeline before turning back to the officiant. "Wait."

"Ray?" Emeline's voice was hardly a whisper, but in the shocked silence of the chapel it rang out clear as a bell.

Ray took a deep breath and turned to her, taking her hand in his. "I can't do this," he said, and I heard an intake of breath from the direction of his parents' pew. "Not to myself. And not to you."

Chapter Seventeen

The silence stretched out while Emeline stared at Ray, lips parted and eyes wide, and all of us stared at the two of them. My breath felt frozen in my chest. *Take the chance*, I wanted to tell her. *Take it and run.*

"This is absurd!"

Every head turned toward the pew where Mrs. Brant was rising from her seat, her expression furious. Emeline looked pale and shaken. Ray's jaw tightened. As I turned I caught sight of Shannon, a pillar of tension, her hands clenched around the bouquet she was holding.

"How could you be so cruel, after all of this? After everything I've done for your family?"

The business merger. I glanced back at Ray's parents, who were also standing, his father a half-step closer to the front than his mother. Her hand rested on his arm like she'd stopped him from closing the rest of the distance between himself and his son.

"Emeline doesn't love me," Ray said quietly. "And you know that, Vivien."

Mrs. Brant's expression twisted. "Of course Emeline loves you," she snapped. "That's just an excuse!"

"It's not." Ray shook his head.

"I see what you're doing." Her voice had dropped to a hiss, but it was still audible. "You want to leave my daughter at the altar, and you don't want anyone to think less of you for it. So you claim that you're doing her a favor. But the truth is that there's someone else, isn't there?"

She took three long steps forward, finger pointed at him like an accusation. "It's that wedding planner girl. She's got her hooks in you."

I shrank low in my seat, heart leaping into my throat, terrified that Mrs. Brant would turn and point me out. But all of her anger was directed at Ray.

"No," Ray said, voice steady. "There is no one else. But I don't love Emeline the way she should be loved. And she doesn't love me. And it's not fair to either of us to go through with this." He looked over his shoulder at his parents, back to Vivien. "Not for money."

There is no one else. I'd thought... I didn't know what I'd thought. He'd told me that he valued the moments between us. Had looked at me like I meant something to him. And yet he stood there saying there was no one else, as though I didn't exist.

Of course he was, I realized. Vivien had already assumed I was the reason the wedding was being called off. If she'd known I was in the chapel, she'd no doubt have turned her anger on me just as sharply as she'd directed it at Ray. He was trying to protect me. A warm little spark lit in my chest.

"How dare you!" Vivien snarled, in the same moment as Ray's father snapped, "Have a little decorum, son." Their voices tangled together, words unintelligible as they both went on.

"Enough!"

The word rang out over the renewed noise in the chapel, and silence fell. Once more everyone turned, this time to look at Emeline, who had finally spoken.

She was pale, but as she stepped out from behind Ray determination was written on her face. Her spine was straight, her shoulders back. It was the same steel I'd seen in her mother, but she didn't bristle with contempt the way her mother always did. In her, that strength was graceful. Elegant.

"Ray is right," she said, firm and decided. "All of this—" She swept her arm out to indicate the candles and the flowers, the sea of faces all watching her. "It's fake. A celebration for something that's completely hollow. And I can't—I *won't* be part of it. Not anymore."

Whispers had started up in the crowd. The bridal party all looked various stages of relieved. Except Shannon, whose expression I couldn't read.

"Emeline," her mother said tightly. "Don't do this."

"Raymond." Ray's father shook off his wife's hand and stepped forward. "We've been planning this wedding for eight months. You don't get to back out now."

Ray turned toward his father, but once again it was Emeline who spoke.

"I'm sorry, Mr. Rose," she said, turning to look at him. "I'm sorry that you went to such expense for this and that it will all be wasted. But even if Ray was willing to reconsider..." She glanced sideways at him, taking a deep breath. "Even if he was, I'm not. We never should have agreed to this wedding in the first place. *I* never should have."

She reached out and took Ray's hands, squeezing them gently. "I'm sorry, Ray. I shouldn't even have accepted your invitation to go out. There may not be someone else for you yet, although—" Her lips quirked briefly into a smile that suggested she knew there was, and knew who. "I'm sure you'll find the right person one of these days. But there *is* someone else for me. There always has been."

Shock crossed Ray's face, and then understanding. Vivien Brant opened her mouth to speak. Ray's father opened his. But Emeline didn't look at either of them. Only turned and, to the sound of gasps from the watching guests, held out her hand to Shannon. The maid of honor dropped the bouquet to take it, her expression open with shock and something like wonder.

And then, while everyone watched, Emeline sank to one knee in her expensive, extravagant wedding gown. Her mother made a sound like a muffled shriek. Ray's father took a step and found his way blocked by James and two of the other groomsmen, who had moved directly into his path and stood staring him down.

"I know I made you wait entirely too long," Emeline said, her voice trembling a little. "But if you still want me, I'm yours from this day forward." She smiled through tears. A dazzling, shining smile. The kind of smile, I thought, that a bride *should* wear on her wedding day. "Shannon Davis, will you marry me?"

The chapel exploded into chaos. Ray's father and Emeline's mother were shouting. Everyone was talking over everyone else. Several people had gotten out of their seats and were demanding answers from anyone who looked involved with the wedding planning, including Nathaniel, who was waving them off with his clipboard and watching the proposal with what I swore were tears in his eyes. And James and the other groomsmen had started up a chant of "Say yes! Say yes! Say yes!" that the bridesmaids quickly joined in on.

Ray looked shell-shocked. But he also, I thought, looked as though pieces he'd been wondering about were finally coming together. And then he turned just enough to catch my eye. My heart skipped a beat. *Can you believe this?* his expression said. I shrugged helplessly, a laugh bubbling in my chest, a smile breaking out on my face. It was... absurd. Absurd, and kind of wonderful. Ray, seeing my smile, made a "What the hell?" kind of gesture, and joined in the chant. I added my voice to his.

Shannon opened her mouth and the room went silent, everyone waiting for her answer.

"Yes," she said. She was crying. Emeline was crying. "Yeah. Hell, Em." She laughed like she couldn't help it, like it was the only outlet for the joy that was filling her from the inside.

"I'll marry you right here if someone will do the ceremony."

Emeline surged to her feet, Shannon helping her rise, and threw her arms around the woman who had been her maid of honor and was now, apparently, her fiancée. A cheer went up around the room as they kissed. Everyone, I thought, would have room for surprise later. Would wonder just what the heck had happened. But for the moment they were all caught up in the story, in the romance of the moment.

Everyone, after all, loves a good fairytale.

Chapter Eighteen

I had almost forgotten about Vivien. Most of us had, I think. At least until she shoved the bridesmaid in her way aside and stalked up to her daughter. Ray's parents seemed to have given up entirely on the situation. They were arguing off to the side, his mother gesturing agitatedly while his father's voice rose with every word. None of us could hear what he was saying, however, because Vivien's shrill fury overrode him.

"You aren't doing this! I won't allow it!"

Emeline broke away from Shannon and turned to look at her mother. "Then disown me," she said flatly.

Vivien stared at her, mouth working, too angry to speak.

"So." Bartholomew said, stepping between the pews and the bridal party. "It seems we've had a bit of a shake-up." He was smiling a little too widely, like he wasn't quite sure how to handle the circus the wedding had suddenly become, but the good humor in his voice sounded genuine. Behind him I could see Nathaniel having a frantic, whispered conversation with Emeline, Shannon, and the officiant. Vivien stood staring blankly at them, like she still couldn't grasp what had just happened. "I guess the good news is there's plenty of alcohol on the island."

Several people laughed, and Bartholomew's smile relaxed a little. Ray's parents, apparently done with their argument, stormed out down a side aisle, the door closing with a slam. I saw Ray's head turn, his eyes following their progress, but he didn't move to go after them.

Nathaniel finished whatever consultation he was having and stepped forward, holding up a hand. The room slowly fell silent.

"You all came here to attend a wedding," he said, looking out over the assembled guests. A grin spread across his face. "So that's what we're going to give you."

The bridal party cheered.

"You can't do that!" Vivien snapped.

"Seeing as I'm the one paying for the wedding," Ray said, stepping forward, "I don't think you have a say in that." He smiled, and he was beautiful. "By all means, Nathaniel. Please continue."

He was, I thought, watching him, such a complete reversal from my last boyfriend. I couldn't imagine Evan's reaction to what had just happened. I didn't want to. But Ray was standing there, genuinely happy to watch the woman he'd just been about to marry wed someone else. And that kindness made me fall for him all over again.

With a little shuffling around, the wedding party—Shannon excepted—took up their places again. The groomsmen seemed to have unanimously decided to stand up with the new bride. The guests sat down. Once more, the ceremony began. Vivien was gone, vanished while everyone was rearranging. Emeline hadn't seemed to notice her absence. I wasn't sure she noticed anything but Shannon, looking up at her with shining dark eyes.

I was distracted from the speech by the rustle of movement beside me, and looked up to find Ray taking a seat. My heart gave a little jump.

"Hey, you," I whispered, low enough that it wouldn't disrupt the vows.

He was close enough that I could feel the warmth of his body next to my own, and then he reached out and wrapped an arm around me, pulling me against his side.

"Hey," he whispered back, his breath against my ear sending a shiver down my spine. "I want you to know, when I said there was no one else..."

"I know," I answered.

He squeezed me a little tighter, and I lay my head against his shoulder. Up at the front of the chapel, the officiant had just asked again if anyone objected to joining of the couple. This time, there was no interruption. Only a look from the bridesmaids that I was pretty sure promised certain death if anyone dared to speak.

"Then," the officiant said, "by the power vested in me, I now pronounce you wife, and wife." A smile slipped into his voice. "You may kiss the bride."

There was a kiss, and applause. Emeline and Shannon were laughing as they broke apart and went down the aisle hand in hand, followed by the bridesmaids. There was a reception still to follow, food and drink and dancing. Ray linked his fingers with mine and smiled at me in the candlelight.

"What do you say we skip the reception and have a little party of our own?"

"I say I like the way you think."

We didn't go out the main doors, where people were lined up to congratulate the newly married couple. There would be time for that later. It was funny, though, I thought as we made our way to one of the side doors, that almost all of the guests had been there for Ray, and now he wasn't even part of the equation. It was going to be a heck of a story to tell when they got back home. The tabloids were going to have a field day. But none of that mattered. What mattered was the heat of Ray's hand in mine, the anticipatory smile he turned toward me as he opened the door. I glanced back over my shoulder as we slipped out, wondering if anyone was watching. The only eyes on us were James'. He gave me a double thumbs up and a huge grin.

"I think I just got your best friend's blessing," I told Ray as he handed me up into a cart. I was reasonably sure it wasn't the one that had brought him, but I doubted anyone was going to be bothered about it. Overhead, the clouds were beginning to break, sunlight spilling down through the gaps onto the cluster of buildings and bringing out the rich color of the flowers tucked amid the greenery.

Ray laughed. "I'm not surprised. If he thought he could get away with it, he'd be trying to steal you for himself. But I guess he decided to take defeat gracefully."

He turned the key, starting the vehicle, and navigated us around the back of the chapel and then down the path that led toward my villa. As we passed the crowd I caught sight of Drew and Ione, shaking Emeline's hand. Bartholomew was standing next to the brides, wearing a beaming grin. Nathaniel, no doubt, was off making sure the details for the reception were set. I faced forward again as the cart picked up speed, and tipped my head back to feel the wind in my hair.

We pulled to a stop in front of my little villa, and both of us were out of the cart and heading up the steps in a moment. At the top, Ray swept me into his arms and carried me over the threshold, smiling down at my shocked laughter, his blond hair falling into his eyes. My breath caught in my chest at the sight. I wanted to tell him he was the best thing I'd ever seen.

What I said was, "I think I love you."

He stopped, stock still, still looking down at me. My chest felt suddenly tight. Had I said the wrong thing? I remembered his grandmother, telling me that he followed his head, that he was afraid to trust his heart. But he had called off the wedding to Emeline. He had come back to me.

"Do you want to know what made me stop it?" he asked.

I blinked at him, not sure where the sudden non sequitur was going. He set me gently on my feet, and took my hands in his own. "The wedding. To Emeline."

Oh. "You told Emeline, didn't you? That you couldn't trap yourself, or her, in a marriage that meant nothing?"

"That was the reason," Ray said. He squeezed my hands. "But that's not why. I stopped because I looked up and saw my grandmother's face." His eyes were locked on mine, intent and so very blue. "You know their story, right? Love at first sight? Grandma told me a long time ago that her mother, my great-grandmother, told her to always follow her heart. To never settle. Not in love, or in anything else."

He looked down at me, eyebrows furrowed. "I told myself for so long that you can't look at someone and instantly love them. That sometimes you have to give up what you want to get what you need. But Violet, I loved you from the moment I saw you sitting there in the passenger seat all windblown and startled by my driving, and you gave me that smile. That gorgeous, delighted smile.

"I've spent every hour since trying to forget the way my heart jumped in my chest right then. But up there at the altar I looked at my grandmother's face, and I thought about love at first sight, and never, ever settling. And so I didn't."

"Ray..." My voice caught.

He smiled. "So, Violet Freesia, I think I love you, too."

I couldn't help it. I had to kiss him. So I did, stretching up on my toes and pressing my lips to his, eager and hungry. He lifted a hand to my cheek and pulled me in deeper, kissing back until we were both breathless and dizzy with desire. There was no desperate longing, nothing wistful in his kiss any longer. Only passion and love and lust and heat.

"Come on." He shrugged out of his jacket, dropping it to the floor in a heap. An instant later his hands were everywhere, tugging my dress over my head, unfastening my bra. I reached for the buttons of his waistcoat and felt his finger slipping under the waistband of my underwear.

"I thought you were the slow-reveal type," I laughed, tossing the waistcoat aside to join the jacket and starting on his shirt.

"That was when I thought I'd never see you again. When I wanted to savor every moment because it was the only one. Now, I want you and I'm not waiting."

He yanked my panties down my hips and a rush of heat went through me at his eagerness. I unfastened his pants as quickly as I could, and stripped him entirely out of the shirt.

"Damn, you're beautiful," he groaned as he stepped back enough to look at me in the grayish light spilling through the window. "I couldn't get you out of my head today."

His fingers trailed down my arms, and then together we made quick work of the rest of his clothes.

He pulled me against him, then, skin to skin, and I melted against the warmth of him, letting him walk me backward until my legs hit the mattress and I tumbled down onto it. He crawled on over me, looking down into my eyes with his hands on either side of my shoulders.

"I could still smell you," he said, leaning close to run his nose along the curve of my throat. I swallowed hard, stomach clenching and need sparking through my core. "When I got back to the room. Getting dressed was the hardest thing I've ever done, because it meant giving up that last fading reminder of you."

His voice was rough with need, and the sound of it woke something desperate inside me. I pulled him down and kissed him, hard and needy. His fingers curled around my hip. I moaned into his mouth.

We came together, that first time, in a rush, impatient, wanting to prove to ourselves that the other was really there. That no one and nothing was going to break us apart this time. His body moved over mine, and I rocked up to meet each thrust. Dragged my nails along his spine and kissed him until neither of us could breathe.

Climax rushed over me like a tidal wave, sudden and all-consuming. As I was swept under, I heard Ray follow me into release. His hands tightened on my thighs. His body shuddered and I shuddered with him, like the same current ran through us both. My vision went white. I thought I called his name, the sound of it ringing off the rafters.

After, Ray lay sprawled on his back beside me, breathing hard. Our fingertips touched. I turned, looking at him, his profile in the early afternoon light, then I rolled onto my side, reaching out to run my finger along his jawline. He caught my hand, kissing my fingers.

"Do you know how happy I am right now?" he asked.

I looked into his eyes, lit from behind by his smile, and leaned forward to steal the taste of that smile with a kiss. His arms went around me, pulling me against him.

"I do," I said when we broke apart. The sound of the surf reached my ears, rhythmic and soft. The air smelled of rain and tropical flowers and salt. And of Ray. I felt joy well up in my chest like light, and thought nothing had ever been so perfect as that single moment. Right there, in a little villa on a Caribbean beach, with the man I loved smiling up at me. "It's written all over your face."

THE END
... Or is it just the beginning?

With This Ring

A TROPICAL STORM-LEVEL romance swirls back to the East Coast. Raymond and Violet find themselves back in Manhattan, caught up in the love they have found for one another.

Tensions are high, and not the good kind. The real world waiting for them isn't as happy to accept their union. Ray's parents are irate. No one approves of Violet. And the worst part of it all is that Ray's career is being threatened by a force that refuses to be unseen. A force that threatens to tank Ray's career as well as Violet's.

Raymond is torn between his family and Violet. She is torn between her happiness and Ray's. And when storms collide, they never mix.

One always wins out, in the end.

Taboo Wedding Series

Book 1 – He Loves Me Not
Book 2 – With This Ring
Book 3 – Happily Ever After
"A romance story yet to be written."

Find Lexy Timms:

LEXY TIMMS NEWSLETTER:
http://eepurl.com/9i0vD
Lexy Timms Facebook Page:
https://www.facebook.com/SavingForever
Lexy Timms Website:
http://www.lexytimms.com

Want

FREE READS?

Sign up for Lexy Timms' newsletter
And she'll send you updates on new releases,
ARC copies of books and a whole lotta fun!

Sign up for news and updates!
http://eepurl.com/9i0vD

More by Lexy Timms:

FROM BEST SELLING AUTHOR, Lexy Timms, comes a billionaire romance that'll make you swoon and fall in love all over again.

Jamie Connors has given up on men. Despite being smart, pretty, and just slightly overweight, she's a magnet for the kind of guys that don't stay around.

Her sister's wedding is at the foreground of the family's attention. Jamie would be fine with it if her sister wasn't pressuring her to lose weight so she'll fit in the maid of honor dress, her mother would get off her case and her ex-boyfriend wasn't about to become her brother-in-law.

Determined to step out on her own, she accepts a PA position from billionaire Alex Reid. The job includes an apartment on his property and gets her out of living in her parents' basement.

Jamie must balance her life and somehow figure out how to manage her billionaire boss, without falling in love with him.

** The Boss is book 1 in the Managing the Bosses series. All your questions won't be answered in the first book. It may end on a cliff hanger.

For mature audiences only. There are adult situations, but this is a love story, NOT erotica.

"**YOUR BRAND. IT'S WHAT you make of it. It's what people say about your company. About you. It's worth everything.**"

Logan Andrews believes in one thing: Money over all else.

So much so that his multi-billion-dollar empire is tanking over it. His ruthless tactics and stone-cold heart have garnered his press his stocks are now paying for. In a few weeks, his billions will be gone if he can't do something about it.

Enter, Mia Charles. An intelligent, beautiful, outspoken woman who specializes in rebranding and repairing media reputations. But once she enters the scene, the only thing Logan can focus on is her lips. Her hips. Her legs. Her curves.

Not repairing the Andrews' name that has already been soiled once.

"HIS BODY IS PERFECT. He's got this face that isn't just heart-melting but actually kind of exotic..."

Lillian Warren's life is just how she's designed it. She has a high-paying job working with celebrities and the elite, teaching them how to better organize their lives. She's on her own, the days quiet, but she likes it that way. Especially since she's still figuring out how to live with her recent diagnosis of Crohn's disease. Her cats keep her company, and she's not the least bit lonely.

Fun-loving personal trainer, Cayden, thinks his neighbor is a killjoy. He's only seen her a few times, and the woman looks like she needs a drink or three. He knows how to party and decides to invite her to over—if he can find her. What better way to impress her than take care of her overgrown yard? She proceeds to thank him by throwing up in his painstakingly-trimmed-to-perfection bushes.

Something about the fragile, mysterious woman captivates him.

Something about this rough-on-the-outside bear of a man attracts Lily, despite her heart warning her to tread carefully.

HE GROANED. THIS WAS torture. Being trapped in a room with a beautiful woman was just about every man's fantasy, but he had to remember that this was just pretend.

Allyson Smith has crushed on her boss for years, but never dared to make a move. When she finds herself without a date to her brother's upcoming wedding, Allyson tells her family one innocent white lie: that she's been dating her boss. Unfortunately, her boss discovers her lie, and insists on posing as her boyfriend to escort her to the wedding.

Playboy billionaire Dane Prescott always has a new heiress on his arm, but he can't get his assistant Allyson out of his head. He's fought his attraction to her, until he gets caught up in her scheme of a fake relationship.

One passionate weekend with the boss has Allyson Smith questioning everything she believes in. Falling for a wealthy playboy like Dane is against the rules, but if she's just faking it what's the harm?

capturing HER BEAUTY
LEXY TIMMS

KAYLA REID HAS ALWAYS been into fashion and everything to do with it. Growing up wasn't easy for her. A bigger girl trying to squeeze into the fashion world is like trying to suck an entire gelatin mold through a straw; possible, but difficult.

She found herself an open door as a designer and jumped right in. Her designs always made the models smile. The colors, the fabrics, the styles. Never once did she dream of being on the other side of the lens. She got to watch her clothing strut around on others and that was good enough.

A chance meeting with one of the company photographers may turn into more than just an impromptu photo shoot.

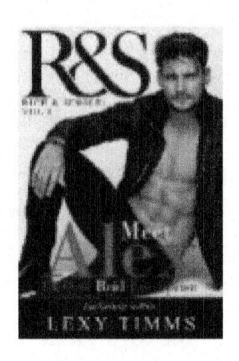

HOT N' HANDSOME, RICH & Single... how far are you willing to go?

Meet Alex Reid, CEO of Reid Enterprise. Billionaire extraordinaire, chiseled to perfection, panty-melter and currently single.

Learn about Alex Reid before he began Managing the Bosses. Alex Reid sits down for an interview with R&S.

His life style is like his handsome looks: hard, fast, breath-taking and out to play ball. He's risky, charming and determined.

How close to the edge is Alex willing to go? Will he stop at nothing to get what he wants?

Alex Reid is book 1 in the R&S Rich and Single Series. Fall in love with these hot and steamy men; all single, successful, and searching for love.

SOMETIMES THE HEART needs a different kind of saving... find out if Charity Thompson will find a way of saving forever in this hospital setting Best-Selling Romance by Lexy Timms

HE LOVES ME NOT

Charity Thompson wants to save the world, one hospital at a time. Instead of finishing med school to become a doctor, she chooses a different path and raises money for hospitals – new wings, equipment, whatever they need. Except there is one hospital she would be happy to never set foot in again—her father's. So of course, he hires her to create a gala for his sixty-fifth birthday. Charity can't say no. Now she is working in the one place she doesn't want to be. Except she's attracted to Dr. Elijah Bennet, the handsome playboy chief.

Will she ever prove to her father that's she's more than a med school dropout? Or will her attraction to Elijah keep her from repairing the one thing she desperately wants to fix?

IN A WORLD PLAGUED with darkness, she would be his salvation.

No one gave Erik a choice as to whether he would fight or not. Duty to the crown belonged to him, his father's legacy remaining beyond the grave.

Taken by the beauty of the countryside surrounding her, Linzi would do anything to protect her father's land. Britain is under attack and Scotland is next. At a time she should be focused on suitors, the men of her country have gone to war and she's left to stand alone.

Love will become available, but will passion at the touch of the enemy unravel her strong hold first?

ASPIRING COLLEGE ATHLETE Aileen Nessa is finding the recruiting process beyond daunting. Being ranked #10 in the world for the 100m hurdles at the age of eighteen is not a fluke, even though she believes that one race, where everything clicked magically together, might be. American universities don't seem to think so. Letters are pouring in from all over the country.

As she faces the challenge of differentiating between a college's genuine commitment to her or just empty promises from talent-seeking coaches, Aileen heads to the University of Gatica, a Division One school, on a recruiting trip. Her best friend dares her to go just to see the cute guys on the school's brochure.

The university's athletic program boasts one of the top hurdlers in the country. Tyler Jensen is the school's NCAA champion in the hurdles and Jim Thorpe recipient for top defensive back in football. His incredible blue-green eyes, confident smile and rock hard six pack abs mess with Aileen's concentration.

His offer to take her under his wing, should she choose to come to Gatica, is a temping proposition that has her wondering if she might be with an angel or making a deal with the devil himself.

THE ONE YOU CAN'T FORGET

Emily Rose Dougherty is a good Catholic girl from mythical Walkerville, CT. She had somehow managed to get herself into a heap trouble with the law, all because an ex-boyfriend has decided to make things difficult.

Luke "Spade" Wade owns a Motorcycle repair shop and is the Road Captain for Hades' Spawn MC. He's shocked when he reads in the paper that his old high school flame has been arrested. She's always been the one he couldn't forget.

Will destiny let them find each other again? Or is what happened in the past, best left for the history books?

** *This is book 1 of the Hades' Spawn MC Series. All your questions may not be answered in the first book.*

BILLIONAIRE BIKER
LEXY TIMMS
Download For
FREE
Lexy
Timms

HOUSE
ROMANCE
CAUGHT
FLAMES
BESTSELLING AUTHOR
LEXY TIMMS
LIMITED
TIME
Lexy
Timms
DOWNLOAD

ONE YOU CAN'T
Forget
LEXY TIMMS
Lexy
Timms
Grab Your
FREE
Copy Today!

Lexy
Timms
THE
BOSS
Lexy
Timms
Grab your
FREE
copy today!

FOREVER
FOREVER
FOREVER
BOOK 3
BOOK 2
BOOK 1
Lexy
Timms
Saving
FOREVER
Lexy
Timms
Limited
Time for
99cents

Bestselling Author
LEXY TIMMS
BEATING THE Biker

LEXY TIMMS
MOMENT IN TIME: BOOK ONE
HIGHLANDERS
Bride

Did you love *He Loves Me Not*? Then you should read *Taking a Risk* by Lexy Timms!

Divorced, childless, and jobless at 30.

My younger self had it all planned. I would be married by 22—check. Have the dream job after university—check. And a couple of kids to go with the perfect wife.

Scratch that.

My wife left me for a guy ten years younger than me, and they're having the babies we should have had. The dream job became a dream when the company I worked for went belly up because of bad investments.

So here I am, moving across the state with just my dog to the big city. Single, jobless and about enough money after the divorce to pay-off my truck, and hopefully rent an apartment.

Apparently it's my destiny.

I got offered an easy job managing some billionaire's estate while he's off to Antarctica for three months on some expedition. So here I sit, counting his money, pretending to be him. Well, more like a glorified house sitter whose German shepherd actually landed me the job because he looks like a guard dog. (Which couldn't be further from the truth.)

What I didn't expect (nor I assume did he) was that his daughter would show up. One that apparently can't stand her father.

He said to treat everything as if it were mine.

I might be taking this job a little too literally.

A "Kind of" Billionaire Series:

Taking a Risk

Safety in Numbers

Pretend You're Mine

Read more at www.lexytimms.com.

Also by Lexy Timms

A Burning Love Series
Spark of Passion
Flame of Desire
Blaze of Ecstasy

A Chance at Forever Series
Forever Perfect
Forever Desired
Forever Together

A "Kind of" Billionaire
Taking a Risk
Safety in Numbers
Pretend You're Mine

BBW Romance Series
Capturing Her Beauty
Pursuing Her Dreams

Tracing Her Curves

Beating the Biker Series
Making Her His
Making the Break
Making of Them

Billionaire Banker Series
Banking on Him
Price of Passion
Investing in Love
Knowing Your Worth
Treasured Forever
Banking on Christmas

Billionaire Holiday Romance Series
Driving Home for Christmas
The Valentine Getaway
Cruising Love

Billionaire in Disguise Series
Facade
Illusion
Charade

Billionaire Secrets Series
The Secret
Freedom
Courage
Trust
Impulse
Billionaire Secrets Box Set Books #1-3

Branded Series
Money or Nothing
What People Say
Give and Take

Building Billions
Building Billions - Part 1
Building Billions - Part 2
Building Billions - Part 3

Conquering Warrior Series
Ruthless

Counting the Billions
Counting the Days
Counting On You

Counting the Kisses

Diamond in the Rough Anthology
Billionaire Rock
Billionaire Rock - part 2

Dominating PA Series
Her Personal Assistant - Part 1
Her Personal Assistant Box Set

Fake Billionaire Series
Faking It
Temporary CEO
Caught in the Act
Never Tell A Lie
Fake Christmas

Firehouse Romance Series
Caught in Flames
Burning With Desire
Craving the Heat
Firehouse Romance Complete Collection

For His Pleasure

Elizabeth
Georgia
Madison

Fortune Riders MC Series
Billionaire Biker
Billionaire Ransom
Billionaire Misery

Fragile Series
Fragile Touch
Fragile Kiss
Fragile Love

Hades' Spawn Motorcycle Club
One You Can't Forget
One That Got Away
One That Came Back
One You Never Leave
One Christmas Night
Hades' Spawn MC Complete Series

Hard Rocked Series
Rhyme
Harmony
Lyrics

Heart of Stone Series
The Protector
The Guardian
The Warrior

Heart of the Battle Series
Celtic Viking
Celtic Rune
Celtic Mann
Heart of the Battle Series Box Set

Heistdom Series
Master Thief
Goldmine
Diamond Heist
Smile For Me

Just About Series
About Love
About Truth
About Forever

Justice Series
Seeking Justice

Finding Justice
Chasing Justice
Pursuing Justice
Justice - Complete Series

Kissed by Billions
Kissed by Passion
Kissed by Desire
Kissed by Love

Love You Series
Love Life
Need Love
My Love

Managing the Billionaire
Never Enough
Worth the Cost
Secret Admirers
Chasing Affection
Pressing Romance
Timeless Memories

Managing the Bosses Series
The Boss
The Boss Too

Who's the Boss Now
Love the Boss
I Do the Boss
Wife to the Boss
Employed by the Boss
Brother to the Boss
Senior Advisor to the Boss
Forever the Boss
Christmas With the Boss
Billionaire in Control
Billionaire Makes Millions
Billionaire at Work
Precious Little Thing
Priceless Love
Gift for the Boss - Novella 3.5
Managing the Bosses Box Set #1-3

Model Mayhem Series
Shameless
Modesty
Imperfection

Moment in Time
Highlander's Bride
Victorian Bride
Modern Day Bride
A Royal Bride
Forever the Bride

Neverending Dream Series
Neverending Dream - Part 1
Neverending Dream - Part 2
Neverending Dream - Part 3
Neverending Dream - Part 4

Outside the Octagon
Submit
Fight
Knockout

Protecting Diana Series
Her Bodyguard
Her Defender
Her Champion
Her Protector
Her Forever

Protecting Layla Series
His Mission
His Objective
His Devotion

Racing Hearts Series

Rush
Pace
Fast

Reverse Harem Series
Primals
Archaic
Unitary

RIP Series
Track the Ripper
Hunt the Ripper
Pursue the Ripper

R&S Rich and Single Series
Alex Reid
Parker

Saving Forever
Saving Forever - Part 1
Saving Forever - Part 2
Saving Forever - Part 3
Saving Forever - Part 4
Saving Forever - Part 5
Saving Forever - Part 6
Saving Forever Part 7

Saving Forever - Part 8
Saving Forever Boxset Books #1-3

Shifting Desires Series
Jungle Heat
Jungle Fever
Jungle Blaze

Southern Romance Series
Little Love Affair
Siege of the Heart
Freedom Forever
Soldier's Fortune

Spanked Series
Passion
Playmate
Pleasure

Spelling Love Series
The Author
The Book Boyfriend
The Words of Love

Taboo Wedding Series
He Loves Me Not
With This Ring
Happily Ever After

Tattooist Series
Confession of a Tattooist
Surrender of a Tattooist
Heart of a Tattooist
Hopes & Dreams of a Tattooist

Tennessee Romance
Whisky Lullaby
Whisky Melody
Whisky Harmony

The Bad Boy Alpha Club
Battle Lines - Part 1
Battle Lines

The Brush Of Love Series
Every Night
Every Day
Every Time

Every Way
Every Touch

The Debt
The Debt: Part 1 - Damn Horse
The Debt: Complete Collection

The Golden Mail
Hot Off the Press
Extra! Extra!

The University of Gatica Series
The Recruiting Trip
Faster
Higher
Stronger
Dominate
No Rush
University of Gatica - The Complete Series

T.N.T. Series
Troubled Nate Thomas - Part 1
Troubled Nate Thomas - Part 2
Troubled Nate Thomas - Part 3

Undercover Series
Perfect For Me
Perfect For You
Perfect For Us

Unknown Identity Series
Unknown
Unpublished
Unexposed
Unsure
Unwritten
Unknown Identity Box Set: Books #1-3

Unlucky Series
Unlucky in Love
UnWanted
UnLoved Forever

Wet & Wild Series
Stormy Love
Savage Love
Secure Love

Worth It Series

Worth Billions
Worth Every Cent
Worth More Than Money

You & Me - A Bad Boy Romance
Just Me
Touch Me
Kiss Me

Standalone
Wash
Loving Charity
Summer Lovin'
Love & College
Billionaire Heart
First Love
Frisky and Fun Romance Box Collection
Beating Hades' Bikers

Watch for more at www.lexytimms.com.

About the Author

"Love should be something that lasts forever, not is lost forever." Visit USA TODAY BESTSELLING AUTHOR, LEXY TIMMS https://www.facebook.com/SavingForever *Please feel free to connect with me and share your comments. I love connecting with my readers.* Sign up for news and updates and freebies - I like spoiling my readers! http://eepurl.com/9i0vD website: www.lexytimms.com Dealing in Antique Jewelry and hanging out with her awesome hubby and three kids, Lexy Timms loves writing in her free time. MANAGING THE BOSSES is a bestselling 10-part series dipping into the lives of Alex Reid and Jamie Connors. Can a secretary really fall for her billionaire boss?

Read more at www.lexytimms.com.

Printed in Dunstable, United Kingdom